The
SIXTH FORM
at
St CLARE'S

D1438081

Have you read these other great books in the *Enid Blyton*™ collection?

Collect them all NOW!

Enid Blyton™

The
SIXTH FORM
at
St CLARE'S

Written by
Pamela Cox

EGMONT

EGMONT

We bring stories to life

First published in Great Britain 2000 by Methuen & Co. Ltd
This edition published 2010
by Egmont UK Limited
239 Kensington High Street
London W8 6SA

ISBN 978 1 4052 1985 3

A CIP catalogue record for this title is available from the British Library

Typeset by Avon DataSet Ltd, Bidford on Avon, Warwickshire
Printed and bound in Great Britain by the CPI Group

Contents

Back to St Clare's

Pat and Isabel O'Sullivan walked along the station platform in a sedate manner, as befitted the head girls of St Clare's. A giggling group of second formers fell silent as they approached, looking at the twins in awe.

'They look nice,' whispered one new girl to her neighbour. 'Who are they?'

'Our head girls – the O'Sullivan twins. And they are nice – very nice.'

The twins heard and shared a secret smile, which held more than a touch of pride. 'Just think of it, Pat. You and I, head girls of St Clare's,' said Isabel. 'I still expect to wake up and find out it was all a dream.'

'More like a dream come true,' said Pat happily. 'And Mummy and Daddy were almost as pleased for us as we were for ourselves.'

'And proud,' laughed Isabel. 'I think Mummy must have rung round all our relations to tell them the news. I half expected her to put an announcement in the local paper.'

'Excuse me,' came a small, lisping voice from behind them. 'Can you help me, please?'

The twins turned and found themselves looking

down at a little girl, so tiny that she looked too young even for the first form, although she wore the school uniform. Pat and Isabel thought her rather sweet, with her halo of golden curls, rosebud mouth and wide blue eyes. They became even wider as they rested on the two identical faces.

'It's all right, kid,' said Isabel with a friendly smile. 'You're not seeing double. We're your head girls, Pat and Isabel O'Sullivan. And who are you?'

'Dora Lacey,' answered the girl. 'I seem to have lost the rest of my form.'

'Come along with us, Dora,' said Pat, putting a hand on her shoulder. 'The first form aren't usually difficult to find. Just follow the noise!'

Certainly the platform from which the St Clare's train was to leave was extremely noisy, as what seemed like hundreds of excited girls milled about, greeting one another loudly and saying goodbye to parents.

'Pat! Isabel! Over here!' The twins looked up and there, coming towards them, was their cousin Alison, along with Hilary Wentworth.

'Hi, twins! Good to see you again,' said Hilary. Then, smiling down at the first former, 'I see you've found a little stray. Miss Roberts is over there some-where, with Bobby and Janet helping her try to round up the first form and herd them on to the train, like sheepdogs.'

'Let's go and help them out,' said Alison, pulling her

heavy winter coat tightly round her. 'I'll be glad when we get on to the train ourselves. At least it should be a little warmer.'

The January day was bitterly cold and many of the girls had already boarded the waiting train rather than stand about on the cold platform.

'Dora!' said the first-form mistress, Miss Roberts, in exasperation when she saw the girl walking towards her with the sixth formers. 'I thought you were on the train already.'

'I was, but I got off again.'

'Well, get back on, and this time stay put!' said Miss Roberts firmly. Then, turning to the twins, 'It hardly seems five minutes since I had you two under my eye as unruly first formers and now here you are, head girls. Well done, both of you. I think Miss Theobald has made an excellent choice.'

'Thanks, Miss Roberts,' said Pat, flushing with pleasure. 'We'll certainly do our best.'

'I'm sure you will,' said Miss Roberts. 'Oh, Lucy, where are you going? That's the third-form carriage! Ours is here.'

'Miss Roberts is certainly going to have her hands full this term,' laughed Hilary.

'Oh, look, here come Bobby and Janet with another group.'

'Hallo all!' called out Bobby and Janet as they shepherded several small girls on to the train. 'Were we this loopy when we were first formers?'

'I suppose we must have been,' said Isabel. 'Though it seems hard to believe now. Dora! What on earth are you doing off the train again? Miss Roberts will skin you alive.'

Somehow, though none of the sixth formers had seen her get off, Dora was on the platform again.

'I thought I might buy some chocolate to eat on the train,' she said, quite unconcernedly.

'You should have done that earlier,' said Pat. 'The train's due to leave at any minute. Hey, Bobby, take this one along to her carriage, would you? And don't turn your back on her!'

'Sweet little thing,' remarked Alison as Dora boarded the train yet again. 'Rather angelic looking.'

Bobby Ellis wasn't so sure. She saw a certain mischievous twinkle in the girl's eyes, recognizing it because it was part of her own nature too. She had a distinct feeling that Dora Lacey could turn out to be more imp than angel.

At last all the first formers were settled, and the twins made their way to their own carriage, where a near-riot broke out.

'Pat! Isabel! Had a good Christmas?'

'Hi, twins! Good to see you both again!'

'Better behave ourselves now that the head girls have turned up!'

'Hallo, Doris . . . and Carlotta! And is that Gladys in the corner?'

Everyone moved along to make room for the twins

and some of the others, who had just come in, Bobby and Janet among them.

'Whew, those first formers are a handful!' said Janet, collapsing on to the seat beside Pat. 'Miss Roberts is going to have her work cut out keeping them in order.'

'Hey, who's that?' said Doris, looking out of the window. 'Must be a new arrival.'

The girls turned and saw a tall, striking-looking girl with long red curls standing on the platform, a sullen expression on her face as she spoke to the man with her.

'That must be her father,' said Gladys. 'Look how similar their colouring is.'

'Well, she's certainly in a temper about something,' said Hilary as the girl scowled fiercely at whatever her father had said. He put his hand gently on her arm and she shook it off angrily, flouncing away to board the train. Just in time, too, as the guard blew his whistle and the journey to St Clare's began.

'Wow, has she got a temper!' exclaimed Alison. 'She looks about our age, too. Let's hope she's not in the sixth.'

'Oh, I don't know. She might be rather exciting to have around,' said Bobby. 'Are we expecting any new girls in our form?'

'Miss Theobald said at the end of last term that there would be a couple,' replied Pat. 'And Priscilla Parsons of the old sixth is staying on. She's too young to leave yet.'

The listening girls groaned. 'You're kidding!' said Hilary. 'I know none of the old sixth form could stand her.'

'No wonder,' said Janet. 'Spiteful, snobbish, interfering – and those are her good points!'

The others laughed. 'Well, we'll just have to set Carlotta on to her if she tries any of her tricks on us,' said Bobby with her wicked grin. 'Remember how she dealt with old Sour Milk Prudence back in the first form?'

The girls laughed as they remembered the wild, fiery little creature Carlotta had been when she first came to St Clare's – all except Carlotta herself. In fact, Pat realized suddenly, Carlotta didn't seem her usual carefree self at all and her normally laughing brown eyes looked decidedly stormy.

'Anything up, Carlotta?' asked Pat in concern. 'Is it the thought of going back to school, or just after-Christmas blues?'

The others stopped their chatter, new girls forgotten as they, too, realized that something was wrong with their friend. Carlotta was a very popular member of the form and if she was in trouble they wanted to know about it, and help if they could.

'Neither,' said the girl, with a shadow of her wide smile, as the concern she saw on the faces around her warmed her a little. 'The fact is, I'm in a mess and I don't know if anyone can help me out of it.'

'Hey, that sounds serious!' said Doris, looking alarmed.

'It is,' said Carlotta. 'You see, my dad has got it into his head – or, to be more precise, my grandmother has *drummed* it into his head – that I need to go to some fancy finishing school once I've finished at St Clare's.'

'But you can't!' cried Bobby, horrified. 'You're coming to university with Janet, the twins and me.'

'That's what I'd *like* to do,' sighed Carlotta. 'Instead I'm supposed to learn elocution and deportment and *cordon-bleu* cookery – which, in my case, will probably be *cordon-bleurgh*!'

'You're not serious!' exclaimed Pat, quite unable to picture the spirited Carlotta fitting in at such a place. 'Finishing school! It'll probably finish you off altogether.'

Carlotta gave a bitter laugh. 'Don't I know it! But Gran's determined that I ought to learn what she calls "social graces".'

'Social graces!' snorted Doris. 'Sorry, Carlotta. No disrespect to your gran, but there are more important things in life than learning how to walk like a model and all that kind of stuff.'

'Right!' agreed Hilary warmly. Carlotta's manners had improved considerably from when she was a wild, uncontrolled first former, fresh from circus life and inclined to fly into a rage at the slightest thing. Her impulsiveness and outspokenness, however, hadn't changed a bit, part of the girl's vivacious personality. And that, thought all the sixth formers, was as it should be. It would be just awful if her individuality was crushed.

'But what's your dad thinking of to agree to such a thing?' asked Alison.

'He always thinks that Gran knows best when it comes to "feminine" matters,' said Carlotta impatiently.

'Girls, help! What am I going to do?'

The sixth formers couldn't bear to hear Carlotta sound so despairing. 'Don't you worry,' Pat reassured her. 'We'll get you out of this somehow.'

'Yes,' put in the quiet little Gladys. 'We'll get up a petition and send it to your father.'

'We'll tell him the rotten finishing school's burnt down,' added Bobby.

'If it comes to it, we'll kidnap you and smuggle you into university with us,' said Janet.

'Even better, we'll kidnap your grandmother,' said Doris quite seriously.

'Idiots!' Carlotta gave a laugh she hadn't thought she had in her. 'Do you know, you've actually cheered me up a bit.'

'Glad to hear it,' said Pat. 'Try not to get too worked up about it. After all, we've a whole year to think up a plan.'

Just then the carriage door opened and there stood little Dora Lacey. 'Oh!' she said blankly, looking surprised.

'Don't tell me,' sighed Isabel. 'You're lost again.'
Dora nodded. 'I just slipped out to the toilet, and when I came back the carriage seemed to have disappeared.' She sighed. 'I'm just not used to finding my own way around. My older sister was supposed to be starting at St Clare's this term too, but she got chickenpox and won't be back for a couple of weeks.'

'That's tough,' said Hilary sympathetically. 'All the same, you ought to be learning to stand on your own two feet a bit now, you know. Your big sister won't want to baby-sit you all the time when she does come to school. Come on.' She stood up. 'I'd better return you to Miss Roberts before she thinks you've jumped off and pulls the communication cord.'

'That bad-tempered-looking girl never joined our carriage after all,' remarked Janet as the door closed behind Hilary. 'Perhaps she's in the fifth.'

'Well, they're a good crowd this term,' said Pat. 'No doubt they'll take her in hand. Pam Boardman's staying down with them, you know. She's to be head of the form.

'I'll miss little Pam, although she was so quiet,' said Isabel.

'Me too,' said Doris in dismay. 'She was my study companion. Now what am I going to do?'

'Oh, well, I guess one of us others will have to put up with your peculiar little ways,' said Alison, earning herself a playful punch on the arm from Doris.

'Doesn't Pauline usually come by train?' asked Gladys.

'Oh, haven't you heard? She's not coming back,' said Bobby. 'Apparently she's decided to take a secretarial course, then she's going to find a job.'

'And Felicity's left too,' said Janet. 'She's to have a long rest before making any decisions about her future.'

Felicity Ray, a musical genius, had been with the girls in the fifth, but had worked so hard at her music that she had driven herself almost to a nervous breakdown.

'Poor Felicity,' said Pat. 'And poor Alma Pudden.

She's to have that operation for her glands soon, so she won't be returning either.'

The girls listened to this with mixed feelings. None of them had liked the plump, pasty Alma with her strange tempers, but once they had learnt that her problems had been due to ill health, they had all felt a little uncomfortable.

'Guess what?' said Hilary, coming back in. 'I've just seen that red-haired girl standing out in the corridor, absolutely sobbing her heart out.'

'She's a little old to be suffering from homesickness,' said Janet scornfully.

'It wasn't that kind of crying,' said Hilary thoughtfully as she took her seat. 'More sort of bitter and angry, as though she had a grudge against the whole world. I went over and asked if I could help, but she turned on me and nearly bit my head off.'

'Wonder what her problem is?' said Bobby.

No one could imagine, and Carlotta said, 'So she could be in our form after all. Who else is still to come back?'

'Claudine, Anne-Marie, Angela and Mirabel,' said Doris. 'I know that Claudine and Antoinette were due to travel back from France yesterday, and presumably the others are going by car.'

'Angela's driving herself,' put in Alison. 'Her folks bought her the neatest little sports car for Christmas. Her dad wasn't too thrilled about it, but you know what Angela and her mum are like once they've set their hearts on something.'

'I didn't know Angela and her mum possessed hearts,' said Carlotta rather maliciously. 'I'm surprised she didn't get her own chauffeur as well.'

Alison, who was Angela's friend, flushed but said nothing. No longer blind to the beautiful, but spoilt, girl's faults, she knew that Carlotta had every reason to sneer at the girl who looked down on her so terribly. The vain, feather-headed Alison had grown up a lot over the past few years, thought Pat, watching her cousin, and was now much more likeable for it.

'Will Angela and Mirabel be coming up into the sixth with us?' asked Hilary 'You know they both failed last term's exams dismally.'

'Mirabel certainly is,' said Gladys, who had spent part of the holidays with her friend. 'And she's to resit the exams. Her dad was so disappointed and gave her a dreadful lecture. The upshot was extra coaching during the holidays, and she's to have some lessons and study periods away from the rest of us so that she can concentrate on her exam work.'

'Yes, Angela's doing the same,' said Alison. 'It's tough on them, just when the rest of us are looking forward to taking things a bit easier after all our hard work last term.'

'Yes,' agreed Hilary. 'I know they brought it on themselves but, all the same, I can't help feeling sorry for them.'

2

The new girls

Claudine, the French girl, waited impatiently for the rest of her form to arrive. She and Antoinette, her third-form sister, had come back to St Clare's that morning, along with their aunt, the French teacher, Mam'zelle. Once they had reported to Matron and been to see Miss Theobald, time had hung heavy on their hands. At last some third formers had arrived and Antoinette had gone off happily with them, leaving her sister to her own devices.

Feeling a little lonely, Claudine wandered off in the direction of the sixth-form classroom, peering inside with interest. 'So,' she mused. 'This is where I shall spend my final year at this very English school. Perhaps it is where I shall, at last, catch the English sense of honour.'

'Hi, Claudine,' said a voice behind her, and the girl turned sharply.

'Anne-Marie!' she exclaimed in delight, then stepped forward and kissed the new arrival on both cheeks in true French style. Anne-Marie was as astonished as she was gratified. She had not been the most popular of girls when she had joined St Clare's last term, being rather pretentious and conceited. Then she had learnt a hard lesson and, as a result, settled down and become a much nicer, more sensible girl. Even so, she hadn't realized that Claudine thought quite so highly of her. In truth, the French girl was so heartily tired of her own company that she would even have welcomed stuck-up Angela, or the loud-voiced, domineering Mirabel.

'*Mon ami*,' she said warmly, taking Anne-Marie's arm. 'What a pleasure it is to see you again.'

'Well, it's nice to see you again, too, Claudine,' said Anne-Marie, quite overwhelmed. 'Did you have a good Christmas?'

'*Oui, très bien*,' said Claudine. 'But it is good to be back, *non*?'

'*Non*. I mean yes,' replied Anne-Marie, becoming confused. 'So this is our new classroom. Not bad, is it?'

Claudine nodded, eyes sparkling. 'Ah, what times we shall have in here, Anne-Marie. What tricks Bobby and Janet will plan. What jokes Doris will make.'

'Yes, but, Claudine, we can't mess about like that now,' objected Anne-Marie. 'We're sixth formers.'

'Oh? And can't sixth formers play tricks and jokes?' asked Claudine, crestfallen.

'Most definitely not,' answered Anne-Marie, shaking her blonde head firmly. 'It's our duty to set a good example to the younger girls.'

'*All* of the younger girls?' said Claudine, dismayed. 'Can we not set a bad example to just one or two?'

'Claudine, you're wicked!' laughed Anne-Marie. 'No, I'm afraid not. We must be well behaved and serious and – well, boring, I suppose.'

Just as Claudine was digesting this, Matron appeared in the doorway. 'Ah, sixth formers,' she said with brisk satisfaction. 'I was beginning to despair of finding any. I've new girl for you here.' She pulled forward a pretty, lively looking girl, with humorous silver-grey eyes and springy blonde curls. Claudine and Anne-Marie took to her at once and exchanged excited glances. 'I'll leave you to get acquainted,' said Matron. 'Must dash – the train girls have just arrived.'

The new girl advanced into the room, betraying not one jot of shyness. 'Hi there!' she said, grinning at the two girls. 'I'm Fizz Bentley.'

Claudine and Anne-Marie stared at her open-mouthed, surprised as much by her Cockney accent as by her unusual name.

'Fizz?' repeated Claudine. 'Surely that is not a real name?'

'No, my real name's Phyllis,' explained the girl with a grimace. 'But my little sister could never pronounce it and called me Fizz, which kind of stuck.'

'It suits you,' pronounced Anne-Marie. 'You look sort of – well – fizzy and bubbly.'

The three girls laughed together at this, which broke the ice completely.

'I've never been to boarding school before,' confided Fizz in the Cockney accent which fascinated the other two. 'But I'm looking forward to it. Do you go in for midnight feasts and that kind of stuff?'

'Alas no, not now that we are so-serious sixth

formers,' said Claudine, mindful of Anne-Marie's words. 'Always we must be so-good and set an example to the younger girls.'

Fizz looked disappointed and Anne-Marie took her arm. 'We'll still have plenty of fun, you'll see. Come on, Claudine, let's show Fizz around a bit before the bell goes for tea.'

The train girls, too, were looking forward to tea after their long journey. Pat and Isabel would have liked to take a look at their new classroom, but there was no time for that. As head girls, they had to go and see Miss Theobald before tea, so they unpacked swiftly before washing their hands and combing their hair. Both girls felt a little nervous as they made their way to Miss Theobald's room. They had had many interviews with the head over the years, but none as important as this, their first as head girls.

'Come in!' came Miss Theobald's clear, calm voice as the girls knocked at her door. She smiled as they entered.

'Twins, how nice to see you again. Refreshed after the break, I hope, and ready to help the mistresses and myself with the running of the school?'

'Yes, Miss Theobald,' chorused Pat and Isabel, liking the way the head made them feel part of her team.

'I don't intend to keep you for very long at the moment, girls,' Miss Theobald continued, 'as I will be addressing the whole of the sixth form after tea in your common-room.'

'Common-room?' repeated Pat. 'Does this mean that

we won't be having our own studies this term?'

'Oh, yes, you won't lose those.' The head smiled. 'But I've a particular reason for wanting you to have a common-room this year as well. There's a large music room along by the studies, which I've had cleared out during the holidays, and it now belongs to the sixth.'

The bell rang just then and Miss Theobald said, 'I'll explain it all to you later, along with the others. Go and have your tea now, and please see to it that everyone assembles in the common-room at six o'clock.'

'Wonder what that's all about?' said Isabel, mystified, as they made their way to the dining-room. 'It'll be a bit of gossip to pass on to the others, anyway.'

Most of the sixth form were already seated round the big dining table when the twins took their places. There was Angela, and Mirabel, both of whom had just arrived by car, and Priscilla Parsons. The sullen girl from the train was there too, so it seemed as though the sixth would have the doubtful pleasure of her company after all. And who was the vivacious-looking girl seated between Claudine and Anne-Marie? She looked like fun. It was so good to be back at school!

The sixth had their tea unsupervised, unlike the younger girls whose teachers sat at the head of each table. Pat and Isabel squeezed in between Doris and Claudine, who immediately introduced the new girl.

'Pat and Isabel, meet Fizz Bentley. Fizz, these are our so-honourable, so-dignified head girls, the O'Sullivan twins.'

The twins grinned at the new girl, at the same time shaking their heads at Claudine.

'Your pronunciation gets worse instead of better,' said Isabel. 'She can't possibly be called Fizz.'

'I am,' put in Fizz herself. 'Honest.'

The twins looked at her in amusement, then Pat stole a glance down the table at the lovely Angela, and nudged her twin. 'See Angela, looking down her nose at the new girl already?' she muttered under her breath. Priscilla looked disapproving too, but by all accounts she disapproved of most people.

'And this is another new girl, Morag Stuart,' said Hilary, who was seated beside the red-haired girl.

'Hallo, Morag,' chorused the twins. 'Welcome to St Clare's.' The girl gave a tight-lipped nod, but said nothing. She had the most stunning green eyes, noticed Isabel. What a pity they were red rimmed from her crying on the train. I bet she'd be really beautiful if only she'd smile, Isabel thought. Well, once she's got to know everyone and settled in, perhaps she'll cheer up a bit.

'*I* should be welcoming *you* to the sixth, twins,' said Priscilla Parsons, with a thin smile. 'After all, I'm the longest serving member of the form, so to speak. If you need any help or advice, don't be afraid to ask, will you?'

'Yes,' murmured Carlotta to Doris. 'If you need any advice on how to look down your nose at people, or listen outside doors, or bully the first formers, Priscilla's a walking information bureau.'

Doris gave one of her sudden, explosive snorts of laughter, which made Priscilla stare at her in astonishment, and Pat's voice trembled with suppressed amusement as she thanked the girl politely. Mirabel grinned too as she caught the twins' eyes and Isabel called out, 'Mirabel! I don't think we've had the chance to speak to you yet – or Angela. Did the two of you enjoy the holidays?'

'Apart from a terrific lecture from my father and some pretty intensive coaching, yes,' answered Mirabel with a rueful grin. 'It made me face up to myself, though, and realize what a prize dope I'd been last term. I'm going to make up for it now, though, and I aim to pass those exams if it kills me.'

The listening girls didn't doubt it. Mirabel was an extremely strong and determined character. Last term, when she had been games captain, she had been a little *too* strong and determined. Power had gone to her head, making her neglect her work and turning many of the girls against her. They were all on her side now, though, admiring her for facing up to her faults and having the courage to try to change herself.

'All wasn't exactly peace and goodwill in our household either,' put in Angela. 'My father reacted much as yours did, Mirabel, and, like you, I'm absolutely determined to pass this time as well.'

The girls were most surprised to hear this from the spoilt, lazy Angela. But there was no doubt that she meant it: she had a determined set to her pretty mouth, which gave her face unexpected character. What a turn-up it would be if Angela made an effort to change her vain, selfish ways and become one of them in her last year. Sadly, such pleasant thoughts were short lived.

'Daddy's promised that, if I pass, I can go to finishing school next year,' went on Angela with a triumphant smile. 'So you can understand that it's absolutely vital I get good results.'

'Trust you!' said Bobby in disgust. 'I would have thought that just passing the exams would have been enough, but you never do anything unless there's something in it for you.'

'Er, just where is this finishing school, Angela?' asked Carlotta in a suspiciously smooth little voice.

'Paris. It's called *St Étienne*,' said Angela, forgetting how much she despised Carlotta in her desire to boast. 'Very exclusive.'

'Of course,' said Carlotta, winking at the twins. 'As a matter of fact, I may well be going there myself next year. Isn't that nice, Angela, to think that you and I won't be going our separate ways once we're finished at St Clare's after all.'

Angela, in the act of sipping her tea, choked, so that Alison had to slap her on the back. Carlotta grinned to herself. There was a bright side to everything.

'*You*!' Angela almost spat out. 'But you can't be! It's for top-drawer people.'

'Well, what's the point of that?' exclaimed Fizz. 'I mean, top-drawer people already know all that etiquette stuff. It ought to be exclusive to bottom-drawer people – like me!'

The sixth formers fell about at this, liking Fizz all the more for making a joke at her own expense. All except Angela, who scowled angrily, and Priscilla, who didn't see anything at all amusing in this common new girl. Angela opened her mouth to make a biting retort, but Isabel saw her spiteful look and stepped in. She wasn't going to allow Angela to pick on a new girl, even though Fizz seemed quite capable of standing up for herself.

'That's enough on the subject for now,' she said firmly. 'Besides, Pat and I have a bit of news of our own.'

'Yes,' said Pat. 'Miss Theobald has turned out the music room along by the sixth-form studies and we're to have it as a common-room.'

'We're to have studies *and* a common-room?' said Anne-Marie in surprise. 'Why?'

'Your guess is as good as mine,' said Pat. 'I think the head has something up her sleeve, though I'm not sure what. Anyway, she wants to speak to us all in the common-room at six, so make sure you're there on time.'

A buzz of excitement broke out at this. Whatever did the head have to say to them? It was all very mysterious – and rather exciting!

3

A meeting with the head

Morag Stuart turned towards the stairs as the sixth form made their way to the new common-room, all of them talking excitedly.

'Hey, Morag!' called Pat. 'Where do you think you're going?'

'To the dormy,' replied the sulky girl in a Scottish brogue. 'I feel like some privacy.'

'At six o'clock? Don't be stupid,' said Pat shortly, sick of the girl's bad temper. 'Didn't you hear Isabel and I say that the head wanted to speak to us all?'

Morag shrugged off-handedly. 'I wasn't taking any notice.'

'Well, you won't get very far at St Clare's if you don't begin to take notice,' said Pat.

The Scottish girl glared at her. 'I don't *want* to get very far at St Clare's,' she said rudely. 'In fact, I'd like to get as far *away* from St Clare's as possible.'

The other girls, who had stopped to wait for Pat, gasped, shocked at her outburst.

'Leave her, Pat,' said Hilary, coming over to lay a hand on Pat's shoulder. 'Let her go if that's what she wants.'

But Pat had a stubborn streak and she wasn't going

to let Morag get the better of her. She had a temper of her own, too, and felt it rising. She couldn't let *that* get the better of her either, or her reign as head girl would be the shortest in St Clare's history. Isabel, who had a calmer temperament, came forward.

'Morag, Miss Theobald has instructed us all to meet in the common-room,' she said with quiet authority, looking the angry girl straight in the eye. 'As head girls, it's our duty to see that her instructions are carried out. Pat and I can't force you to come along but, if you refuse, we'll have no alternative but to report you to the head.'

Morag scowled ferociously. She had met Miss Theobald briefly on her arrival and, although she would rather die than admit it, was more than a little in awe of her. With one last scorching glare in Pat's direction, she turned away from the stairs and joined the others. Pat blew out her cheeks. Well done, Isabel!

'Thanks,' she said gratefully to her twin. 'You handled that perfectly. I was in great danger of completely losing my temper.'

'I could see that,' said Isabel with a grin. 'And that would have put you in the wrong. I know Morag's annoying, Pat, but I don't think that getting mad with her is the answer.'

Pat bit her lip and nodded, feeling a little ashamed of herself now. 'I didn't expect to lose my temper so early in the proceedings,' she said woefully.

'Don't worry about it,' said her twin, giving her a

clap on the arm. 'You got it under control again, that's what matters. And just because we're head girls doesn't mean that we're perfect and don't have faults, the same as everyone else. We just have to try to deal with them. Now, let's get a move on – I'm dying to see our common-room.'

'Very nice,' said Alison as they entered. 'Smells of new paint, though.'

It was certainly a pleasant room, newly decorated in a warm, peach shade. A large, rectangular table stood in the centre, surrounded by chairs, and more comfortable armchairs were dotted about the place.

'I must admit, I quite enjoyed having a common-room when we were lower down the school,' said Doris. 'It's great to have our studies and a little privacy, but it's nice to be able to all get together and have a good gossip too.'

'Looks as though we're going to get the best of both worlds,' said Gladys, looking round. 'Great, there's a record player and a radio!'

'I much prefer the peaceful atmosphere of the studies,' put in Priscilla heavily. 'I always feel . . .' But the girls were never to find out what Priscilla felt, because Anne-Marie, who was by the door, hissed, 'The head's coming!'

Immediately everyone lined up on one side of the big table and Miss Theobald entered.

'Good evening, girls,' she said with her pleasant smile. 'Please sit down.'

The sixth form sat, but Miss Theobald remained on her feet for a few moments, looking from one watchful face to another. 'It's nice to see you all together – those that have come up through the school from the first form, and a couple of new faces, too.' She smiled at Fizz and Morag, though the latter averted her eyes and did not smile back. The head looked at her intently for a moment, then continued, 'No doubt most of you have guessed that I've asked you here for a specific purpose and I'll come to that in due course. But first, it's my pleasant duty to announce the appointment of the new games captain.'

The girls looked at one another eagerly. Who would it be? Bobby or Janet, perhaps? Both were brilliant at sports. Probably not Hilary, as she was leaving at the end of term. Certainly not Alison or Claudine, both of whom hated games and got out of playing whenever they could. Mirabel bit her lip. It wouldn't be her, either. She'd had one stab at the job and made a complete mess of it.

'This wasn't an easy decision to make,' said Miss Theobald. 'The job requires a little more than an aptitude for sports – determination, patience, sportsmanship – and a good sense of humour! Well, many of you possess those qualities, but in the end Miss Wilton and I decided on . . . Gladys Hillman!'

Gladys turned bright red, looking round her in total disbelief while the girls congratulated her noisily, reaching across to pat her on the back. She was absolutely thrilled – but how would Mirabel feel about it? She glanced at her friend and Mirabel smiled warmly.

'Congratulations, Gladys,' she said. 'You deserve it and I know you're going to do a fantastic job.'

The head smiled at Mirabel's generous words and was pleased. The girl had much better stuff in her than she had shown last term. She held up her hand for silence and got it immediately.

'Bobby and Janet are to be joint vice-captains,' said the head. 'I'm sure that the three of you will work well together.'

Bobby and Janet exchanged delighted glances. Both took a keen interest in games and got on very well with Gladys.

'And now to the main business of the evening,' said Miss Theobald. 'As you know, St Clare's is growing all the time. This term there are more girls than ever in the two lowest forms and the mistresses find that they don't have as much time to spare for the girls' problems and worries as they would like. That's where you come in.' She paused to look round the table, and the girls stared back keenly, their curiosity thoroughly aroused. 'I want you to hold a weekly meeting in here,' she explained, 'to which any girl from the lower school can bring her worries and problems and talk them through with you. Most of you are sensible, responsible girls, and I know I can trust you to act in the best interests of the young ones.'

The girls looked at one another feeling quite

overwhelmed. What an honour, to be entrusted with a responsibility like this. And they were all determined to prove worthy of it, to do their best for the younger girls and the school.

'Of course, they must go to their form mistresses with any difficulties concerning schoolwork,' continued Miss Theobald. 'And there may be times when serious matters come to light that you feel should be reported to the mistresses or myself. But I'm sure you all know what I expect of you, without me having to draw up a list of rules. Angela and Mirabel, as you will both be working hard for your exams, neither of you will take part in the meetings for the time being.'

Angela, who had little time for anyone's problems but her own, looked unconcerned, but Mirabel was bitterly disappointed. Why had she been so stupid last term?

Miss Theobald saw her unhappy expression and said gently, 'I'm not excluding you as a punishment. But when you take time off from your studies I want you to use it to relax, not to bother over someone else's worries.' The head paused, looking directly at Mirabel, then at Angela. 'I also think it would be a good idea if the two of you shared a study until the exams are over.'

The two girls, who didn't get on at all well together, looked horrified, as did Gladys and Alison, who had been their study-mates in the fifth.

'I don't normally interfere with study allocation, but as you share a common purpose this term, it might be less distracting for you to be with one another rather than with your chosen friends.'

'Yes, Miss Theobald,' agreed both girls without enthusiasm. Angela glared at Mirabel. Loud, bossy, arrogant – she would never survive cooped up with her.

Mirabel glared right back. Of all the girls in the school, the last one she would have chosen to share with was that little madam.

'That's all I have to say,' said Miss Theobald, rising. 'I'll leave you to talk over what I've said, then if you all go along to Matron she will allocate your studies. Carlotta, I'd like a quick word with you in my room.'

'Of course,' said the girl politely, though she was a little surprised. Whatever could the head have to say to her? She followed Miss Theobald from the room, the girls beginning to chatter excitedly as soon as the door closed behind them.

'Well, I wasn't expecting this!' cried Pat.

'I'm vice-captain,' said Bobby, grinning all over her face. 'Janet, I'm vice-captain!'

'I know, dope,' laughed Janet. 'So am I, remember? This term's going to be the greatest!'

'You bet,' agreed Hilary. 'I wonder what the head wanted with Carlotta, though?'

She soon found out, for the girl returned a few minutes later.

'Come on,' Isabel said to her. 'It's time we went off to Matron to get our studies sorted out. You'll be sharing with Claudine again, I suppose?'

'I wish!' Carlotta took a quick glance round the room and lowered her voice, saying, 'The head has asked me to share with Morag.'

'*Morag*!' said Doris loudly, and Carlotta gave her a little push.

'Shh, idiot, she'll hear you.'

'But why Morag?' asked Doris more quietly. 'That's not going to be much fun, especially after sharing with someone as wacky as Claudine.'

'I can't say that I'm looking forward to it,' said Carlotta wryly. 'Miss Theobald thinks that I may be able to help Morag to settle in here. She reckons that I was very much like her when I first came to St Clare's.'

'No way!' said Hilary indignantly. 'You were *hot* tempered, Carlotta, not *bad* tempered like she is.'

'I don't think that's quite what she meant,' said Carlotta thoughtfully. 'I think she meant that we're alike in that I had trouble settling in here as well at first. Miss Theobald wouldn't tell me why Morag hates being here so much, of course. Part of the plan is that I try to encourage her to confide in me.'

'Well, I don't envy you,' said Pat, looking across at the Scottish girl who was staring broodingly out of the window.

'It'll be quite an achievement on your part if you can bring her round and turn her into one of us,' said Hilary. 'She really is hard work.'

'Well, I've given the head my word that I'll do my best,' said Carlotta. 'Oh, and she gave me a bit of good news too.'

'What?' asked the others curiously.

'Apparently Dad wrote to her, asking her to give me a reference for this finishing school,' Carlotta told them. 'And Miss Theobald doesn't think it's a good idea for me to go there at all. She's promised to speak to Dad about it on my behalf.'

'Great!' cried Doris. 'Trust Miss Theobald!'

Carlotta felt hopeful, too. Her father had the greatest respect for the wise and kindly headmistress. If anyone could change his mind, she could.

'You'd better go and break the news to Claudine that she'll have to find someone else to share with,' said Pat, nodding towards the French girl who was having an animated conversation with Fizz. 'I expect she'll be disappointed.'

Claudine was, for she had enjoyed sharing with Carlotta in the fifth form, but she accepted the news with a shrug. 'You must do what you think is right, *ma chère* Carlotta. Me, I wish you luck. That Morag, she is – how do you say – bristly.'

'Prickly,' Carlotta corrected her with a grin. 'She sure is. I'm glad you aren't offended because I'm not sharing with you, Claudine.'

Claudine seldom took offence at anything. Besides, she had taken a great liking to Fizz and decided to ask her to share. And so the sixth form paired off. Pat and Isabel shared, of course, as did Bobby and Janet. Fizz happily agreed to go in with Claudine. Alison approached Gladys, saying with her pretty smile, 'How about you and I teaming up, seeing as we've both lost our study-mates?' Gladys, who had feared that she might end up with Priscilla, said yes at once. She liked Alison, although the two of them didn't have a great deal in common. Doris and Hilary paired up too, which left Anne-Marie with Priscilla. Poor Anne-Marie wasn't at all happy, but felt a bit better when Doris whispered, 'Cheer up! Don't forget that Hilary will be leaving at the end of this term, then you can move in with me. Until then, just try to grin and bear it.'

Looking at Priscilla's tight, prim face, Anne-Marie felt that grins were going to be in short supply that term. And Carlotta hadn't fared much better, stuck with that miserable Morag. Of the two girls, Anne-Marie wasn't sure who was worse.

The girls went along eagerly to inspect their new studies. Each was furnished with a table and two armchairs, but the girls could add their own individual touches by bringing items from home. It was also a custom of the school that they could call on the first formers to do any small jobs for them. As they shut their door behind them, the twins remembered how they had felt this was beneath them when they had started at St Clare's.

'What a couple of idiots we were – the stuck-up twins!' laughed Isabel, recalling the name given to them by their class.

'Yes. Thank goodness we woke up to ourselves and realized what a great school St Clare's is,' said Pat.

'Otherwise we certainly wouldn't be head girls now.'

'It doesn't bear thinking of,' said Isabel with a shudder. 'Shall we go back to the common-room, or be by ourselves for a while?'

'Let's stay here for a bit, just the two of us,' said Pat, drawing up an armchair by the fire and snuggling down into it contentedly. 'Mm, this is nice. It'll be great having tea in here by ourselves on cold, dark evenings.'

'Lovely,' agreed Isabel, taking the chair opposite her twin and yawning. 'I'm bushed. I suppose the train journey and all today's excitement has worn me out. What time is it?'

'Only eight o'clock,' said Pat, looking at her watch. 'I don't think I'll be staying up late tonight, though.' The sixth formers were allowed to set their own bedtime, within reason.

'Me neither,' sighed Isabel. 'Much as I'd like to. There's so much to talk about. The new girls, for example. I think Priscilla and Morag are going to test our tempers this term. I like Fizz though, don't you?'

'She's great,' agreed Pat. 'Even though she's so different from the rest of us, she's good for a laugh. Generous, too.'

Fizz had produced an enormous chocolate cake at tea-time, generously sharing it with the whole table. Even Angela and Priscilla had accepted some. Only Morag had refused a slice with a curt, 'No, thank you,' but as she had eaten very little at all no one thought too much of it.

'I wonder what she's doing at St Clare's, though?' said Isabel.

'Isabel O'Sullivan!' exclaimed Pat, shocked. 'What a snobbish thing to say! I'd expect a remark like that from Angela, but not from you.'

'I didn't mean that she *shouldn't* be here,' Isabel said, ruffled. 'I thought you knew me better than that, Pat! I just wondered what made her folks suddenly decide to send her here in her final year. And did you see her clothes? Every bit as expensive as Angela's.'

'Mm, I noticed,' replied Pat. 'But I don't think there's any big mystery about Fizz. She's an open book and no doubt she'll tell us all about herself in her own good time.'

'I guess so,' Isabel said. 'Pity we can't say the same about Morag. She's all defensive and closed up somehow. I don't know about you, Pat, but I reckon that with the new girls and our weekly sessions with the kids, we're in for a pretty exciting term.'

Neither she nor Pat could begin to imagine just how exciting!

4

The first day

The twins slept well on their first night as head girls, waking bright and early next morning.

'Morning, Carlotta!' called out Pat, smiling at the tousle-haired girl opposite as she sat up sleepily.

'Hi, Pat.' Carlotta yawned, stretching like a cat. 'These early starts are going to take some getting used to after the long lie-ins during the holidays.'

'Mm,' agreed a sleepy voice from the next bed, as Hilary raised her head. 'And these dark mornings make it so much harder. In summer I actually *want* to get out of bed.'

'Well, there's someone who doesn't mind getting up, even on a morning like this,' joined in Isabel, nodding towards the bed nearest the door, empty and unmade.

'Morag!' exclaimed Hilary. 'Pat, you don't suppose she's done a bunk, do you?'

'Wow, I hope not!' said Pat, biting her lip. 'I wouldn't fancy having to explain to Miss Theobald that we've lost one of the new girls already.'

But as the girls began to get out of bed, the door opened and in came Morag, dressed in trousers, sweater and a warm jacket.

'Where have you been?' asked Isabel sharply.

'For a walk in the grounds.' She scowled defiantly at Isabel. 'There's no rule against that, is there?'

Pat and a few of the others glared at her. All of them felt an intense loyalty to their school and didn't like the way this newcomer seemed to mock their rules and traditions.

The girl went across to her bed and took off her jacket, before brushing out her long, red hair, which had become rather windswept. Just then a bell went, and those girls who hadn't yet risen climbed out of bed, with much groaning. Seeing that Fizz looked a little bewildered, Pat said to her kindly, 'That's the dressing-bell. In about twenty minutes it'll be breakfast time. Haven't you been to boarding school before, Fizz?'

'No, I went to the local day school,' answered the girl. 'And it was nothing like this.'

'What made your folks decide to send you to St Clare's?' asked Hilary, not feeling in the least awkward about asking such a personal question. There was something warm and open about Fizz that made you feel as if you'd known her for years. The girl glanced round and took a deep breath, before announcing, 'My dad inherited stacks of money. Millions, in fact. A relative we didn't even know about died, and Dad was the sole benefactor.'

All the girls crowded round, listening intently now, Bobby exclaiming, 'Wow, that must have been just great! But didn't you want to stay on with your friends at your old school?'

Fizz sighed. 'People started to change towards me once we moved into a big house and they heard what had happened. Suddenly I came in for a lot of spiteful remarks, even from girls I'd thought were my best friends. Everyone expected me to change and go all snobbish. Suddenly I just didn't fit in any more. I just hope that I'll fit in here.'

'You bet you will,' chorused the others, liking her open manner.

'Yes, we'll take care of you,' said Janet.

'You'll probably come up against a bit of spite from the Honourable Angela,' added Carlotta with her wicked grin. 'But don't take it personally – she looks down on all of us.'

Everyone laughed. Angela, Alison and some of the others were in the dormitory next door, and the girls couldn't wait to tell them Fizz's exciting news.

'Come on, everyone!' called Pat. 'Let's move it! We don't want to set a bad example to the young ones by being late for breakfast on the first day.' She glanced across at Morag, who had now changed into her uniform, and called out, 'Aren't you going to do your hair, Morag?'

'I've just brushed it.'

'Yes, but we're supposed to wear it tied back in class. Either that or cut short.'

Morag shrugged. 'I never wear my hair tied back.'

Pat frowned. The girl certainly had lovely hair, but Miss Harry, the sixth-form mistress, was unlikely to appreciate its beauty if Morag went into class with it

35

tumbling about her shoulders like that. Pat was about to say so, quite bluntly, when Carlotta said softly, 'Leave her. Let her make a few mistakes. After all, we can't put her right until she does something wrong.'

'You *are* getting wise in your old age,' grinned Pat. 'All right, but I bet Miss Harry will go nuts when she claps eyes on our flame-haired beauty.'

The sixth form was filing into its new classroom when Bobby happened to spot a lone, small figure hovering in the corridor.

'Hi, Dora!' she said with a smile. 'What are you doing here? This is the sixth's classroom, you know. Don't tell me you're lost again?'

Dora Lacey nodded.

'Well, the quickest way to the first-form room is for you to go back along the corridor, out of the side door, then cut across the courtyard and in through the door by the Science Lab. Got that?'

'I think so,' lisped Dora, looking doubtful.

'Do you want me to walk you over?' offered Bobby kindly.

'No, I'll be all right. Thanks.' And with that the girl sped off, leaving Bobby grinning ruefully and shaking her head. That kid was badly in need of some geography lessons!

Going into the sixth-form room, Bobby placed her books on her desk, then glanced out of the window, what she saw making her eyes widen in amazement. 'Unbelievable!' she cried. 'I've never seen anything like it!'

'What?' asked the others in surprise.

'That first former, Dora. I left her outside that door seconds ago, and there she is now going across the courtyard. She must have run like a cheetah to have covered that distance in a few seconds.'

'She'll be one to watch at netball practice then,' said Gladys, ever the games captain. 'She's got definite possibilities if she's that fast.'

Then the girls heard the sound of brisk footsteps and became silent, those that were seated getting to their feet as their new form mistress, Miss Harry, entered.

'Morning, girls.' She smiled round the room. 'Please sit down, then we can get to know one another.'

The sixth formers liked Miss Harry, who was young and pretty with a great sense of humour. She also understood that her pupils were growing up fast and liked to be treated as young adults rather than children. But any girl who mistook Miss Harry's good nature for a lack of authority had better watch out! She soon learnt her mistake and never repeated it.

'Now, obviously I know some of you better than others,' the mistress began. 'But I'd like you all to stand up, one at a time, and introduce yourselves. That will help both me and the new girls – oh, and Priscilla, of course, to get to know you.'

Priscilla, who had chosen a desk at the front of the class, stretched her thin lips into a smile, which Miss Harry studiously ignored. Having already had the girl in her class for two terms, she knew a great deal about

Priscilla and, try as she might, could not like her.

'We'll go in alphabetical order,' said the mistress, glancing at the list in her hand. 'Starting with Phyllis Bentley.'

Fizz, quite taken aback by how young Miss Harry looked, stared with fascination at the teacher, but neither moved nor spoke.

'Fizz!' hissed Claudine, her neighbour. 'It is your turn.'

'Oh, sorry, Miss Harry,' apologized Fizz in her strong accent, blushing as she stood up. 'I'm not used to answering to Phyllis, you see. Most people call me Fizz.'

Had this been the first or second form, the girls would have burst out laughing at this. The dignified sixth stifled their amusement and merely grinned at one another. All except Priscilla, whose expression grew sour. That girl! Didn't she realize that it just wasn't done to ask a mistress to use a nickname? And such a stupid one! Priscilla sat back and waited for Miss Harry to deliver a crushing put-down. But the mistress was smiling. Something about Fizz's direct, open manner was very appealing. 'Fizz it is, then,' she said with a twinkle in her eyes.

'Carlotta Brown?'

Carlotta got up and, with a theatrical bow, introduced herself.

Priscilla's mouth became so small and mean it was in danger of disappearing altogether. What *was* St Clare's coming to, she thought disapprovingly. Carlotta didn't belong here, any more than that common Bentley girl.

Everyone knew that Carlotta had once belonged to a circus. As for Claudine – Priscilla cast a disdainful glance at Mam'zelle's daredevil niece and shuddered – if only the school was more selective about who was accepted here. Shrewd Carlotta watched her from the corner of her eye as she sat down, guessing at the girl's thoughts and despising her for them. Priscilla was the kind of person she hated most. Everything about her was thin and mean, from the shape of her face, to her long, narrow nose which, so rumour had it, she enjoyed poking into everyone's business. Even her hair was braided in a long, thin plait, more suited to a first former than one of the older girls. Yes, Carlotta was going to have her work cut out this term keeping her temper with both Prim Priscilla and Miserable Morag. Yet keep it she must. Not only was the honour of the sixth at stake, but her own future. If her father had any reports of bad behaviour, he would be more convinced than ever that she needed a course at finishing school.

Morag also watched the proceedings, but with total contempt. She didn't want to get to know these carefree, sensible girls with whom she had nothing in common, and she didn't want them prying into her business, trying to turn her into one of them. When the time came for her to stand up, she would let the class know in no uncertain terms that she wanted no part of St Clare's. Perhaps Miss Harry would report her, and no doubt that interfering Pat would tell her off, but Morag didn't care. She had been forced to come here, and certainly wouldn't abide by St Clare's rules. Arms folded, she sat back in her seat as, one by one, the girls took their turn. Then, at last, it was hers.

'Morag Stuart!' called out Miss Harry.

The girl got to her feet, the familiar scowl on her face. 'I'm Morag Stuart, and I don't want . . .'

'One moment!' interrupted Miss Harry, frowning. 'Morag, you seem to have forgotten to tie your hair back this morning.'

'I didn't forget,' replied Morag brusquely. 'At home I always wear my hair like this, and . . .'

'Well, you're not at home now,' Miss Harry said with her air of quiet authority. 'Please go up to your dormitory and do your hair properly.'

Morag narrowed her eyes. 'I don't want to tie my hair back.'

'Fine,' said the mistress unexpectedly. 'You're quite old enough to make up your own mind, and the choice is simple. There is an excellent hairdresser's in town, and if you refuse to keep your hair tied back during lessons, I suggest you pay a visit there and have it cut short.'

'Cut short?' repeated Morag, aghast.

'Yes, I think it would suit you,' said Miss Harry with a smile. 'You have a very pretty face, Morag. It would be nice to see *all* of it, rather than just catching a glimpse of it through a curtain of hair now and then.'

Morag reddened. Somehow her defiant stand had gone horribly wrong and she had merely ended up looking stupid. Far from voicing her opinion about

St Clare's, Miss Harry had barely allowed her to get a word in.

'Well, Morag?' said the mistress now. 'What's it to be?'

The sullen girl was dying to answer back, but something in Miss Harry's direct, blue-eyed stare and the firm tone of her voice stopped her. Without quite knowing how it had come about, Morag suddenly found herself outside the classroom and on her way up to the dormitory. Well done, Miss Harry, thought the class admiringly. She certainly knew how to handle the bad-tempered Scottish girl. And well done, Carlotta, thought Pat. She had foreseen what would happen and had had the good sense to stop Pat from interfering.

The sixth form had their heads bent over their work when Morag reappeared a few minutes later, a blue ribbon confining the red hair. Softly, so as not to distract the others, Miss Harry called her over to her desk and explained what the class was doing. She really *is* attractive, thought Isabel, glancing up. What I wouldn't give for those lovely, high cheekbones! Only the sulky droop of her mouth spoilt her. As though sensing eyes on her, Morag looked round sharply and Isabel gave her ready, friendly smile. Suddenly, without wanting to, Morag found herself smiling back, warmed to see a friendly face. Then she remembered the course she had set herself and switched the smile off. But Isabel was a little heartened as she turned her attention back to her work. At least the girl *could* smile. Besides, Miss

Theobald obviously thought she was worth a little trouble, otherwise she wouldn't have encouraged Carlotta to befriend her. And if the head thought so, that was good enough for Isabel.

5

Sixth formers and first formers

When afternoon lessons were over, Pat and Isabel, along with Hilary and Doris, went to the common-room to draft a notice concerning what had become known as their 'agony aunt' sessions. It had been decided to wait until the third week of term to hold the first meeting, giving everyone a chance to settle in properly. Then the weekly meetings would be held on Thursday evenings at seven o'clock, and a notice was to be placed in each common-room to let everyone know.

'Isn't this exciting?' said Doris. 'I can't wait for our first meeting.'

'Yes, we just *have* to make a success of this,' said Pat earnestly. 'It's quite a responsibility Miss Theobald's given us and we have to prove that we're up to it.'

'Well, we *will* prove it,' said Isabel determinedly. 'If we haven't learnt how to be responsible and make decisions after six years at St Clare's, there's not much hope for us.'

'There are some people who never learn, though,' put in Doris.

'Priscilla!' said the others at once.

'Yes, we'll have to watch her,' Hilary said. 'She's

likely to use the sessions as a chance to find out the kids' secrets and snitch on them.'

'As soon as she starts anything like that, she's out!' said Pat. 'We'll have to keep an eye on Morag, too.'

'Morag?' repeated Isabel in surprise. 'I know she's not exactly Little Miss Sunshine, but she doesn't strike me as nosey, or a sneak.'

'No, but she obviously cares nothing for St Clare's or its traditions,' Pat pointed out. 'And we don't want her passing on those ideas to the younger girls.'

'Ah, what is this?' asked Claudine, opening the door. 'Have I tripped on a secret meeting?'

'You mean stumbled on, Claudine,' laughed Doris. 'No, we were just discussing our "agony aunt" sessions. Do you mind taking one of these notices along to Sarah in the second form? Tell her to put it up in the common-room and make sure everyone reads it.'

'*Eh bien*,' agreed Claudine, taking the sheet of paper from Doris and whisking herself from the room.

'Hilary, you and Doris go to the third's common-room,' said Pat. 'Isabel and I'll shoot along to the first form.'

'Come on, then,' said Isabel. 'I'm dying for a coffee, and the sooner we get this over with, the sooner we can get back to our study and put the kettle on.'

As they were leaving the common-room, they bumped into Dora Lacey and Pat called out, 'Dora! Be a pet – nip into our study, put the kettle on and spoon some coffee into a couple of mugs, will you? You'll find some chocolate biscuits in the cupboard as well. Help yourself to a couple. Only a couple, mind – I've counted them!'

'Will do, Pat!' The first former laughed and ran off, leaving Isabel staring doubtfully at her twin. 'I hope you know what you're doing. She's a sweet kid, but dippy. We'll probably get back to find the socket burnt out or something.'

But, by the time the twins reached the first-form common-room, Dora was there, curled up on the sofa reading a magazine.

'Dora!' exclaimed Pat in astonishment. 'Have you got motorized shoes or something? I've never known anyone move as quickly as you do.'

'Is everything OK?' asked Isabel anxiously. 'I mean, you found the kettle and everything?'

For a moment Dora looked blank, then her brow cleared and she said, 'Oh, the kettle! No problem, Isabel.'

'OK, girls, listen up!' called out Pat. 'Isabel and I have an announcement to make.'

But Isabel said nothing, staring at Dora with a puzzled frown on her face as Pat told the first form all about the weekly meetings, delighted when they were full of enthusiasm for the idea.

'Leave me to do all the talking, why don't you!' cried Pat, when they got outside. 'What's up with you?'

'Dora Lacey,' answered her twin slowly. 'Something about that kid just isn't right.'

'What do you mean?' asked Pat, surprised.

'I can't put my finger on it. But something just doesn't add up where she's concerned.'

Alison and Gladys had also sent for a first former, Joan Terry, to do their jobs. Gladys had slipped out to speak to Miss Wilton, the games mistress, when the girl arrived, and Alison greeted her with a wide smile. 'Hi, Joan! Put the kettle on and we'll have a cuppa, then you can help me find a home for this lot,' she said, busily emptying the contents of a cardboard box on to the table. 'Fudge – ugh! I used to love it when I was a kid, but I can't stand it now. Trouble is, my gran still thinks I'm a kid and sends me a box every term.'

Joan giggled. She was slightly timid and usually very much in awe of the older girls, but Alison was so friendly that she nerved herself to suggest shyly, 'Can't you tell her that you don't like it any more?'

'I couldn't,' said Alison. 'That would hurt her feelings terribly and, much as I hate fudge, I'd hate to hurt Gran's feelings even more. Do you like fudge, Joan?'

'I love it. Mum doesn't have much money to spare, so I don't often have sweets sent to me.'

Alison was touched. Joan was thin and plain, but there was something wistful and appealing about her that went straight to the girl's tender heart. 'Here, catch!' She tossed the box of sweets to Joan. 'And don't eat them all at once. I don't want Matron after me because you've been sick or come out in spots or something.'

'Thanks, Alison,' breathed the younger girl, her

grave brown eyes sparkling. 'What do you want me to do now? Shall I find a place for these books?' Alison was really nice, she thought. She had put her completely at ease. Gladys, who came in just before Joan left, was nice too. Joan had always pictured games captains as being large, domineering and loud. So it was a pleasant surprise when Gladys said in her soft voice, 'I hope we'll be seeing you at netball practice tomorrow afternoon?'

'You bet! I've never played before, though, so I hope you're not expecting too much.'

'Don't you worry about that,' said Gladys. 'If there's potential in you, we'll bring it out all right.'

Joan almost danced from the room and along the corridor, clutching the box of sweets as though it contained the crown jewels. Before she had gone more than a few steps, she ran smack into Priscilla Parsons. 'Sorry, Priscilla,' she stammered. 'I wasn't looking.'

'Evidently,' snapped Priscilla, her sharp eyes on the box Joan carried. 'Where did you get that from?'

'Alison gave it to me.'

'Are you sure?' said Priscilla, leaning forward so that her gaze bored into Joan's. 'Quite sure that you didn't . . .'

At that moment Alison put her head out of the study and said, 'Joan, would you . . . oh, Priscilla.'

'Alison.' Priscilla gave a tight smile and inclined her head. 'Joan here was just telling me that you'd given her this box of fudge.'

'That's right,' said Alison, taking in the younger girl's scared expression. Whatever could Priscilla have been saying to her? She felt a sudden wave of dislike and said, with unusual sharpness, 'Not that it's any of your business. Did you want something?'

Priscilla turned red, answering stiffly, 'No, I was just on my way to my study.'

'Well, don't let us keep you,' said Alison rudely and, after shooting her a glare, Priscilla stalked off. Joan gave a little sigh of relief and Alison frowned. She wasn't a very shrewd girl, but she was sensitive to the feelings of others and knew that something was wrong here.

'Do you know Priscilla well?' she asked gently.

'Quite well,' replied Joan. 'We live in the same village.'

'Tough luck,' Alison said with a grimace. 'It's bad enough having to put up with her during term time, never mind during the holidays as well.'

It really wasn't done for one of the top-form girls to speak against another to a member of the lower school but, thought Alison with a surge of rebellion, it was worth it to see Joan smile. She still looked a little wan, though, and Alison said kindly, 'You know, if you ever come up against any bullying, or there's anything troubling you, the sixth are here to help. Just come along to one of our Thursday sessions.' Then she remembered that Priscilla would be present at these sessions and added hastily, 'Or just come and have a word with me in private. My door's always open.'

Joan looked at Alison as though she were some

kind of goddess and said shyly, 'Thanks.'

Alison smiled. 'Now, what was I going to say before Priscilla so rudely interrupted us? Ah, yes, I was just going to ask if you'd like to come along tomorrow at the same time and give me a hand sorting out the rest of my stuff.'

'Sure,' said Joan eagerly. 'I'd love to.'

Meanwhile, Priscilla had gone to her study, pleased to find that Anne-Marie was not there. Sly and secretive by nature, Priscilla would have much preferred a study to herself. Moreover, having been in the sixth for two terms already, she thought herself superior to most of the old fifth formers, and Anne-Marie was no exception. Priscilla admired Angela because the girl was upper class and came from a wealthy family. And she would have liked to make friends with the twins, not because she liked them, but because they were head girls and it would have been pleasant to bask in their reflected glory. The twins, though, had shown clearly that they had little time for Priscilla. But the girl refused to be downhearted. There were still the Thursday night meetings to look forward to, and that appealed to her sense of self-importance enormously. Like the others, she was impatient for the first meeting. But, unlike Hilary or Bobby or Janet, Priscilla didn't think of what an honour it was to be entrusted to help the lower forms with their problems. She thought what a brilliant way it would be to find out their secrets. And if she could manage to use those secrets somehow, that would be even better. Yes, Priscilla meant to make her presence felt this term all right.

The following afternoon, Gladys, Bobby and Janet went along to watch the first formers at netball. Hilary, who took a keen interest in sports, accompanied them, and the twins, who were busy, promised to come along later.

'Susan's pretty good,' said Bobby, watching the girl move swiftly up and down the court.

'She is,' agreed Gladys. 'But then she should be, because she's been playing for a couple of years. I'm keen to see how the girls who are new to it shape up.'

Some played well, picking up the rules quickly, whilst others were slow to take to this new game. Joan Terry seemed hopeless, but when Janet suggested trying her as goalkeeper, she proved quite adept at knocking the ball away from the net.

'Good one, Joan!' called out Janet. 'Hey, Gladys, I think we've a future goalkeeper here.'

Gladys nodded, writing hurriedly in the notebook she had brought with her.

'Here's Dora,' said Bobby. 'I wonder what kind of a showing she'll make?'

The girl made a very good one, learning the rules swiftly and obviously enjoying herself as she darted all over the place, passing the ball agilely.

'Wow, she might be small, but she's good!' Gladys cried. 'And she's not afraid to tackle her opponent, even though Hilda's so much taller.'

By half-time Gladys had listed several good players who could possibly be put into a team later on. 'Brilliant!' she smiled happily at Bobby and Janet. 'I've a feeling St Clare's are going to do well at netball this term. Hey, Dora, where are you off to?'

'Stone in my shoe,' called back Dora. 'Don't worry, Gladys, I won't be long.' She was back in time for the second half, but her play had deteriorated. And she seemed to have forgotten most of the rules, too. Gladys, Bobby and Janet exchanged puzzled glances. Pat and Isabel arrived just then and, watching Dora, Pat said, 'She's fast, but that's about all you can say for her.'

'Yes, but she was playing so well in the first half,' said Gladys with a frown. 'Bobby and Janet will bear me out.'

'That's right,' Janet confirmed. 'But she seemed to go to pieces after half-time. Almost as though she'd lost her memory and forgotten everything she'd learnt.'

Miss Wilton took Dora aside and patiently explained the rules to her again, after which Dora's game improved dramatically and she even scored a goal.

'Well, Gladys, what do you think?' asked Miss Wilton, coming off the court. 'Joan Terry showed promise in goal and Dora . . . well, I don't quite know what to make of her.'

'Perhaps when she knows the game better she'll settle down,' said Gladys. 'At the moment she's a little unpredictable.'

'Yes,' agreed the games teacher thoughtfully. 'The change seemed to occur at half-time. When she came back it was as though she was a different girl!'

A big surprise

On Saturdays, the girls were free to do as they chose, many of them going into town to spend their allowances, or to see a film. It happened that the twins' grandmother had sent them some money, so they decided that a visit to the coffee shop was in order that afternoon. As they were getting their jackets, they bumped into Anne-Marie, looking the picture of misery.

'It's the thought of listening to Priscilla droning on and spreading poison about half the school over tea,' the girl explained when Pat asked her what was wrong. 'I'll be sorry to see the back of Hilary at the end of term, but it'll be Heaven to move in with Doris!

'Come with us,' invited Isabel, feeling sorry for Anne-Marie. 'We're going out to the coffee shop.'

'Yes, do,' said Pat. 'They do the best toasted sandwiches I've ever tasted.'

'Don't tempt me!' groaned Anne-Marie. 'It sounds great and I'm starving, but I can't. It's Mum's birthday *and* my little brother's next week, so all my allowance had to go on presents for them.'

'Our treat,' said Isabel generously. 'Pat and I are well off at the moment.'

'Thanks, girls, but I couldn't let you,' said Anne-Marie firmly.

'Sure you could,' said Pat with equal firmness, getting down the girl's jacket and handing it to her. 'Come on, I'm starving!'

So, delighted to be over-ruled, Anne-Marie slipped on her jacket, and soon the three girls were seated on high stools in the window of the coffee shop, enjoying toasted ham and cheese sandwiches washed down with large milkshakes.

'You were right, Pat – these are great!' said Anne-Marie, taking a large bite of her sandwich. 'And it's so nice to have your company after Priscilla. I'll return the favour once I get next month's allowance, that's a promise.'

It was as the twins went to the counter to pay that Anne-Marie saw something odd. Glancing out of the window, she spotted a small, familiar figure going into the bookshop opposite. That looks like little Dora, she thought, then frowned. Surely she hadn't been silly enough to come into town alone? There was a strict rule at St Clare's that the lower forms could only visit the town if they went in pairs. Only the fifth and sixth formers had the privilege of going alone if they wished. The first former would really be in trouble if the head or Miss Roberts – or even the twins – got to hear about it.

Staring out of the window, wondering whether she ought to mention the matter to Pat and Isabel, Anne-Marie's eyes widened. For there, going into the same bookshop, was Dora – *again*! The sixth former blinked and rubbed her eyes. How could that be? Anne-Marie hadn't looked away from the shop doorway for a second, and Dora certainly hadn't come out. So how could she have gone in a second time?

'Hey, Anne-Marie, you look as though you've seen a ghost!' said Pat as the twins returned to the table.

'Well, I've certainly seen something weird,' said the girl, and quickly told them her strange tale.

'Your eyes must have been playing tricks on you,' said the down-to-earth Pat. 'I expect the second girl you saw resembled Dora. After all, there are quite a few first formers with blonde hair.'

But Anne-Marie remained adamant that it was Dora she had seen and suddenly Isabel, who had been frowning thoughtfully, slapped the table. 'I've got it!' she cried. 'Pat, do you remember me saying the other day that something didn't add up about that kid? Well, I've suddenly realized what it is. She was able to tell both of us apart straight away.'

'So?' Pat said, puzzled.

'Well, you know as well as I do that most people can't. Not immediately. It usually takes them a while.'

'That's true,' put in Anne-Marie. 'I know when I first met the pair of you it took me a few weeks before I realized that your hair curls a little more than Pat's, Isabel, and that her eyebrows are just a tiny bit straighter than yours.'

'Exactly!' said Isabel triumphantly. 'But when we

spoke to Dora the other day, she called us both by our names and got them right.'

'Well, I suppose it is unusual,' Pat agreed, frowning. 'Normally the only people able to do that are other identical twins because they are so used to looking for minute differences between themselves and their own twin. Isabel! Surely you're not suggesting . . .'

'That's *exactly* what I'm suggesting!' broke in Isabel impatiently. 'I think there are *two* Doras!'

'It would certainly explain a lot,' said Anne-Marie, who had been listening open-mouthed. 'Like how she turns up unexpectedly so often, and moves from one place to another with such speed.'

'Right,' agreed Isabel. 'It would also explain her strange performance on the netball court yesterday. One twin must have played the first half, and the other the second.'

'The little monsters!' exclaimed Pat. 'No wonder Dora did our jobs so quickly the other day and managed to get back to the common-room in record time!'

'What are we going to do about it?' asked Anne-Marie, thoroughly astounded by the whole business, but relieved to know that there was nothing wrong with her eyesight.

'First we've got to get the pair of them out of that bookshop,' said Pat grimly, getting to her feet. 'Then, I'm afraid, we've no alternative but to take them to Miss Theobald.'

'Anne-Marie, you stand guard outside,' said Isabel as they crossed the road. 'Pat and I'll go in, and if either of them tries to sneak out, grab her!'

But there was no need for such measures for, as the twins were about to enter the shop, the door opened and two identical girls emerged, coming to an abrupt halt as they looked up into the stern faces of their head girls.

'Well?' demanded Pat crisply. 'What have you two got to say for yourselves?'

'It – it was just a joke, Pat,' stammered Dora – or was it her twin?

'One that may have got you into serious trouble,' said Isabel sternly. 'Which twin are you?'

'I'm Dora,' said one, hanging her head.

'And I'm Daphne,' her twin added.

The three sixth formers studied the girls closely, searching their faces for any difference, however small, that would tell them apart. The Lacey twins had tricked them once, but they were determined not to be fooled again.

'Daphne's eyes are a slightly deeper blue than Dora's,' pronounced Isabel at last. 'And she's just a fraction taller. All right, kids, now we're taking you back to St Clare's.'

'Will you have to tell the head?' asked Daphne, lip trembling as Isabel took her arm.

'I'm afraid so,' said Pat, doing likewise with Dora, as Anne-Marie brought up the rear. 'You'll get into trouble but, honestly, you really have asked for it. However have you managed to get away with it for a whole week?'

'Nothing to it, really,' said Dora, not without a touch of pride. 'I just forged a letter from Mum saying that Daphne was ill and wouldn't be able to start school for a fortnight, then sent it off to Miss Theobald.'

'Just a minute,' interrupted Isabel with a frown. 'I distinctly remember you saying that your *older* sister was coming to St Clare's.'

'Daphne *is* my older sister,' explained Dora righteously. 'She was born half an hour before me, so I wasn't lying! Only Miss Theobald and Miss Roberts knew that we were twins, though, and they didn't suspect a thing.'

The O'Sullivans and Anne-Marie exchanged glances and had to bite their lips to keep from laughing. There was something so innocent and appealing about the twins, even when they were owning up to the most outrageous behaviour.

'We've been taking turns going to lessons and having meals,' Daphne put in. 'And we've been sharing the bed in our dormitory. Dora would have it one night, while I slept on an old mattress in one of the box-rooms, then the following night we'd swap.'

'Yes, but *why*?' asked Anne-Marie, completely at a loss.

'It just seemed like a good idea,' they said in unison.

Pat and Isabel could understand this more readily than Anne-Marie. As first formers they, too, had enjoyed confusing both girls and teachers. They had never gone this far, though, and it was unlikely that the head would look upon this as a mere joke.

'Do you realize what would have happened if your folks had decided to telephone Miss Theobald to see how you were both settling in?' asked Pat sternly. 'There would have been a full-scale panic and the police would have had to have been informed that one of you was missing. Imagine how worried your mum and dad would have been.'

'We didn't think of that,' said Dora, looking ashamed.

'It seems to me that the pair of you didn't think at all,' scolded Isabel. 'Well, here we are, back at St Clare's. Take a good look at that roof, twins. Any minute now, Miss Theobald is going to go right through it!'

The younger girls' faces crumpled suddenly and they began to cry. Anne-Marie, although she thought that they had behaved irresponsibly, felt sorry for them and whispered, 'Pat, Isabel – need we report them to Miss Theobald? Couldn't we pretend that Daphne's just arrived on the train, having recovered from her illness?'

'Absolutely not!' said Pat firmly. 'Those kids deserve what's coming to them. Besides, if it did all come out later, as these things have a habit of doing, Isabel and I would probably lose our positions as head girls for not reporting it.'

'Pat's right,' Isabel agreed. 'If they get away with this, who knows *what* they might decide to do next!'

'I suppose so,' sighed Anne-Marie. 'Going into town with you two certainly isn't boring, I'll say that much!'

In the entrance hall the girls ran into Mam'zelle, who greeted them with a beaming smile. 'Ah, how good it is to see you big girls taking charge of the little ones,' she said warmly. 'The dear little Dora, is it not? And who is this behind her?' Mam'zelle's beady black eyes grew round in amazement, glasses slipping down her nose a she rubbed her eyes, much as Anne-Marie had done earlier. '*Mon dieu*, what is this?' she cried, putting a hand to her heart. 'My eyes, they are deceiving me!'

'I'm afraid it isn't your eyes that have been deceiving you, Mam'zelle,' said Isabel drily. 'But these two.'

Briefly, the girls told her the facts. The French teacher was quite horrified. Dora Lacey, although her French wasn't good, had swiftly become one of the teacher's pets, being just the kind of sweet, angelic-looking girl who appealed to her. To discover that she had been tricked by one of her favourites was too much! '*Méchantes filles*!' she cried. 'To think that you two – so young, so innocent – should be so wicked. Ah, the good Miss Theobald, she will be truly angry, and rightly so.'

The Frenchwoman suddenly seemed very frightening to the twins who, having just dried their tears, promptly began to cry again. As swiftly as it had come, Mam'zelle's anger vanished. She put a plump arm about each of the twins' heaving shoulders, saying kindly, 'Do not cry, *mes petites*. You will be punished, yes, but soon all this will be forgotten. Then you will settle down and be good, good girls, *n'est-ce pas*?'

The twins nodded, giving watery smiles, and the French mistress patted their rosy cheeks.

'We'd better take them along to the head now,

Mam'zelle,' said Isabel politely, hiding a smile at the teacher's swift change of mood.

'Of course. Miss Theobald will be just, *mes filles*, do not fear. Bear your punishment nobly.' And with these words of wisdom, she went on her way.

'Dear old Mam'zelle,' laughed Pat fondly as she watched the Frenchwoman shuffle away in her large, flat shoes. 'No matter how often she's tricked, she always forgives. Anne-Marie, are you coming to the head with us?'

'No, I'm going for a quiet sit down in the common-room,' said the girl, moving away. 'I've had quite enough excitement for one day.'

'Well, it's not over for us,' said Isabel. 'Come on, kids – time to face the music!'

7

More secrets

Miss Theobald's charming smile of welcome for Pat and Isabel turned to an expression of concern when she saw their grave faces. 'Is something wrong, twins?'

In answer they pulled forward Dora and Daphne, who had been cowering behind them, wishing that the ground would open up and swallow them.

'Daphne, I presume!' exclaimed the head in surprise. 'Your mother didn't ring to let me know that you would be back so early. I hope you're fully recovered?'

'Excuse me, Miss Theobald,' said Pat. 'But Daphne hasn't just arrived. The two of them have been here right from day one.'

Out came the full story of the Lacey twins' outrageous deception. The head's face grew more and more stern as she listened.

'Well!' she exclaimed at the end. She had been head of St Clare's for many years and had dealt with all kinds of strange situations, but never one like this before. 'Thank you, Pat and Isabel,' she said seriously. 'You can go now – and I'm grateful to you for handling this matter so responsibly and for bringing it to my attention.'

Then, as the door closed behind the head girls, she

turned her stern grey eyes on the two first formers, both of whom were shuffling uncomfortably and feeling very small. 'Never have I come across such reckless and irresponsible behaviour,' she told them coldly. 'You have deceived the teachers, the other girls and your parents. How do you suppose they would feel if they heard about your behaviour?'

'Oh, Miss Theobald, *must* you tell them?' pleaded Daphne, her mouth trembling. 'We never meant any harm, honestly. It was just a joke.'

'A joke that could have misfired badly,' said the head. 'How can the school offer you its care and protection if no one knows you are here? Imagine if a fire had broken out during the night, Daphne. Only your twin would have known that you were missing and where to find you.'

What a horrifying thought! Shivers ran down the twins' spines as they stared at one another, appalled.

'Whether or not I tell your parents depends upon the two of you and your behaviour for the rest of the term,' went on Miss Theobald. 'I believe that you meant no harm and this exploit was, in your eyes, just a bit of fun. However, you must both learn to think things through, consider the consequences of your actions and accept responsibility for them. That is one of the things your parents have sent you here to learn.' And the head intended to see that they learnt it well! 'You are both grounded for a fortnight,' she said. 'Also, as you have each only been taking half of your lessons, you will do an extra half-hour's prep every evening for a fortnight. Now, I want you both to go along to Miss Roberts and own up to her. Whether or not she chooses to impose any further punishment of her own is entirely her decision.'

'Wow!' said Dora, once they were outside the head's room. 'That was awful! My knees are still knocking.'

'Mine too,' said Daphne glumly. 'Grounded for two weeks! That's just terrible! I only hope that Miss Roberts doesn't give us a punishment too.'

Miss Roberts didn't, but she was absolutely furious and her anger was not as controlled as the head's had been. She always hated to be duped in any way, and the ears of the two first formers burnt by the time she had finished with them. Of course, the news of Dora and Daphne's escapade spread through the school like wildfire. Although Katie, the serious head of the first form, addressed a few measured words to them, most of their class were absolutely thrilled at their daring, and the twins almost became heroines to them. 'Which is only going to encourage them in further tricks,' remarked an exasperated Miss Roberts to Mam'zelle in the mistresses' common-room.

'Ah, but surely they have now learnt their lesson,' said Mam'zelle. 'They will soon settle down.'

'I wish I had your confidence, Mam'zelle,' sighed Miss Roberts. 'Well, we'll see.'

The twins, carrying out their dreaded punishment, did their best to be good, as they both hated to be confined to school. And as for an extra half-hour's prep every night . . . well, that was enough to make *anyone* think twice before stirring up trouble. Only one lapse occurred to mar their attempts at good behaviour, and that was caused by Priscilla Parsons who, spotting them in the corridor near her study one afternoon, took it upon herself to lecture them. As Dora said to Daphne later, she didn't mind being shouted at by the head girls. She didn't even resent the telling-off that Katie had given them. They were doing their duty and had the twins' welfare at heart. But Priscilla didn't. Her sole motive for scolding the girls was a love of interfering and airing her opinions. Dora and Daphne listened to her in gathering anger, feeling none of the shame or fear that had overcome them when the O'Sullivan twins had caught them out. 'I'll be keeping an eye on you both,' finished Priscilla heavily. 'And if I catch you doing anything you shouldn't be . . .'

'You'll tell on us!' said Daphne with a sneer. 'Well, you keep your eye on us, Priscilla, but you'll have nothing to report. Because Dora and I are too smart for you. Whatever we plan, you'll never find out about it until it's too late.'

'Oh!' gasped the older girl. 'How dare you?' She was furious and humiliated by their nerve, knowing that the twins wouldn't dare speak in such a way to any other sixth former, and she felt resentful of the fact that she wasn't treated with the same respect. Priscilla couldn't understand that even the youngest first former could see right through her pompous, self-righteous manner to her spiteful nature, and for this reason she would never gain the respect of the younger girls.

'What are you doing here anyway?' she asked sharply, trying to regain her dignity. 'These are the sixth form studies, you know.'

'We do,' answered Dora insolently. 'Claudine and Fizz asked us to come along and do a few jobs for them. If they ask why we're late, Priscilla, we'll explain that you kept us.'

The girl flushed angrily. Just then, Joan Terry rounded the corner and Priscilla's eyes lit up spitefully. Here was one first former she could bully easily. 'Joan!' she called out bossily. 'Come here!'

Hunching her shoulders, Joan came across and said meekly, 'Yes, Priscilla?'

'I was just telling the twins here that it's time they settled down and stopped playing stupid tricks,' said Priscilla smugly. 'Don't you agree?'

Poor Joan shifted uneasily from one foot to the other. What could she say? On the one hand she didn't want to fall out with the twins, who she sincerely liked, besides greatly admiring their audacity. On the other, she couldn't afford to offend Priscilla, who knew so much about her family. Unable to look at Dora and Daphne, the girl said tonelessly, 'Yes, Priscilla.'

The sixth former smiled triumphantly while the twins glared at Joan's bent head. 'Well, off you go then,' she ordered, and Joan scuttled thankfully away to Alison's study.

'Are you all right, Joan?' asked Alison in concern, thinking that the girl looked a little pale and worried.

'I'm OK, Alison,' said Joan, managing a little smile. 'I just bumped into Dora and Daphne, and couldn't help wishing I was more like them.'

'Well, I'm glad you're not!' said Alison with feeling. 'Pair of brats! No, Joan, I think you're just fine the way you are.'

Joan cheered up enormously, basking in these words of praise as she got happily to work. What did the twins and Priscilla matter so long as her idol, Alison, liked her as she was?

Dora and Daphne, meanwhile, were having a great time in Fizz and Claudine's study. The two older girls had been highly amused by the story of the twins' deception and were eager to hear all about it first hand.

'Ah, you bad girls!' Claudine teased them with a twinkle in her eye. 'I almost wish that I was in the first form so that I could share in your jokes and tricks.'

'I don't know how the pair of you had the nerve!' exclaimed Fizz. 'Weren't you afraid you'd be caught?'

This was music to the twins' ears, coming on top of Priscilla's hard words, but irresponsible of Fizz and Claudine. It was one thing for the sixth formers to laugh amongst themselves about the younger girls' exploit, but quite another to encourage them openly. Claudine, more versed in the ways of boarding school than Fizz, said as much when the twins had left.

'If Pat or Isabel knew how much we had laughed

with the younger girls they would think it most undignified of us,' she explained to Fizz. 'It is better that we say nothing to the others.'

Fizz looked thoughtful and, oddly for her, a little serious. 'I wonder how the sixth would like it if a member of their own form was keeping a secret from them,' she remarked at last.

'*Ma chère* Fizz, it is not to be thought of,' said the French girl, throwing up her hands in pretend horror. 'We sixth formers do not deceive or play tricks on one another. We are good, we are . . .'

'Yes, but what if someone was deceiving them for a good reason,' interrupted Fizz. 'Surely they wouldn't mind then.'

Something in the girl's tone made Claudine look at her sharply. 'Do not tell me that you, too, have a twin hiding somewhere in the school?' she said. 'It is surely not possible that I have been sharing my study with *two* Fizzes!'

Fizz laughed. 'No, there's only one of me.'

'Then why do you ask me such a question?' Claudine said suspiciously. 'You have a secret, Fizz, I know it! Come, you must serve the beans!'

'Spill the beans, dope!' laughed Fizz. 'Oh, Claudine, I don't know if I should.'

'But of course you should!' exclaimed the French girl. 'Me, I love secrets and I am so, so good at keeping them.'

Fizz studied Claudine's mischievous little face for a

moment and decided that she could trust her. The French girl had her own sense of honour, although it was a little different from the English one. Also, she had a love of the dramatic and mysterious which meant she would enjoy guarding her friend's secret.

'All right, Claudine,' said Fizz, taking a deep breath. 'I'll tell you.' So she told. And Claudine listened, silent for once, her eyes round and mouth agape.

'*C'est incredible*!' she gasped at the end, then gave a deep laugh. 'Priscilla and Angela will be so, so furious when they find out.'

'Yes, but I don't want *anyone* finding out just yet,' Fizz said firmly. 'This is between the two of us, Claudine.'

'And it shall remain so,' promised Claudine solemnly, putting a hand on her heart. 'Upon my honour.'

The first formers were laughing and chattering in their common-room, some of them dancing to music on the radio, others reading and some just enjoying sprawling around doing nothing in particular. The Lacey twins were arguing noisily over possession of a magazine when the door opened and they fell silent, drawing together as Joan Terry entered.

'Traitor!' called out Dora, giving the girl a scornful glance.

'What are you doing here, Joan?' asked Daphne. 'Tired of hanging round with the sixth form?'

'Hey, what goes on?' asked Katie, taking in the twins' contemptuous faces and Joan's pale, scared one. Some of the other girls gathered round to listen as well.

'She sided with Priscilla when she told us off earlier,' explained Daphne indignantly.

'I didn't!' protested Joan. 'But I couldn't very well argue with a sixth former, could I?'

'You could have stuck up for us a bit,' said Dora. 'But you don't seem to think much of the first form. Always hanging round that silly Alison O'Sullivan.'

'Alison isn't silly!' said Joan at once, her cheeks becoming hot.

'See! You'll defend her, but not us, your own classmates,' sneered Daphne. 'Traitor!'

'Stop it!' said Katie, looking worriedly from the twins to Joan. The first formers were, on the whole, a happy crowd and she didn't want any petty quarrels boiling up to spoil things. 'Twins, you have to learn that it isn't always easy for some of us to stand up to the likes of Priscilla,' she said with great wisdom. 'And don't forget that you always have one another for support, whereas the rest of us – like Joan – are on our own.'

Dora and Daphne listened to Katie, who they liked and respected very much, and bit their tongues.

'As for you, Joan,' she went on. 'We all know how unpleasant Priscilla can be, but she can't be allowed to get away with her sneaking and her bullying, sixth former or not. If you can just bring yourself to stand up to her a bit, we'll all back you up and be proud of you.'

Joan nodded but her thoughts were bleak. Katie's advice was sound but the girl didn't know Priscilla like she did. Nor did Katie know all about Joan, as the sixth former did.

'Something else, Joan,' said Katie, taking Joan's arm and leading her a little apart from the others. 'How about making some friends in our form? We're not a bad bunch on the whole, you know, and although Alison's really nice, you're just a kid as far as she's concerned and she can't really want you hanging round all the time.'

'OK, Katie,' said the girl listlessly. She didn't add that most of the first formers weren't interested in making friends with her because they found her quiet and boring. That was her own fault, she knew. But she hadn't always been that way. Once she had been fun-loving and happy, just like the others. Until everything had gone horribly wrong. Alison was different, though, in spite of what Katie said. She liked Joan and was kind to her. Who cared what Katie, the twins and the rest of the first form thought? Joan would stay where she was wanted – with Alison!

8

Morag in trouble

As the days went on, those members of the sixth who had come up through the school together felt as though they had never been away. Fizz, too, settled down quickly, popular with everyone but Angela and Priscilla. Whenever either of them were around, the girl took great pleasure in exaggerating her Cockney accent and talking in the strangest rhyming slang, most of which, the girls were sure, she made up as she went along. The standard of her work was high, as she had a quick intellect and only needed to look at a page to memorize it. Alison and Doris who, no matter how hard they worked, were consistently bottom of the class, envied her ability to achieve excellent results with the minimum effort. 'I can't help wondering how our Cockney sparrow will get on in French,' Pat had said with a chuckle. 'Her accent's sure to be terrible!'

But Pat had been wrong. Not only was Fizz well-grounded in the rules of French grammar, her accent was almost as perfect as Claudine's.

'At last!' Mam'zelle had cried in delight. 'Someone who speaks my language as she should be spoke. *Très bien, ma petite.*'

It was fortunate that Claudine didn't have a jealous nature, as Mam'zelle, already much taken with the girl's good looks and bubbly personality, made a great favourite of Fizz. Morag Stuart, on the other hand, was not a success. Her work was well below the standard of the sixth and she made no effort to improve. She was so rude and inattentive that Miss Harry actually threatened to send her out of the room one day, something unheard of for a sixth former. The rest of the girls had been horrified, as the disgrace would have reflected badly on the whole of the class.

'Ah, this Morag, she will turn my hair grey and white!' exclaimed Mam'zelle one day, when the girl had been particularly difficult. 'Never will you learn to roll your Rs in the French way. You are a great big stupid! Even more stupid than Doris.'

Doris, who was totally useless at French, though she could imitate Mam'zelle's accent to perfection for the amusement of the girls, grinned round the class. Morag scowled. Carlotta sighed. She was finding sharing a study with the girl very trying. Morag never initiated any conversation, responding to Carlotta's attempts with forbidding, one-word answers. Forthright Carlotta, in the habit of speaking her mind, often found it difficult to control her temper. But if she blew up and told Morag exactly what she thought of her, it would be impossible for the two of them to continue sharing, and she would feel that she had let Miss Theobald down. Morag had clashed with Pat several times too, and

Carlotta could see a terrific row boiling up there.

Things came to a head after netball one morning. Games was the one thing Morag shone at and the only lesson she appeared to enjoy. She was strong and agile, and seemed able to work off some of her aggression in the gym, or running around outside. This was the first time she had played netball, but she took to it immediately. She was a natural player, fighting fiercely for possession of the ball and sticking to Pat, the girl she was marking, like glue.

'She can certainly play,' said Bobby to Gladys. 'You'd never guess this was her first time.'

Gladys nodded. 'She needs to be more disciplined, though. Look at the way she barged into Pat just then! If this was a school match, she would have been sent off for that.'

As it was, Miss Wilton blew her whistle and took Morag aside to deliver a few measured words. Sadly for Pat, the girl ignored them! A few minutes later Hilary threw the ball and Pat, breaking away from Morag, ran to catch it. The Scottish girl wasn't far behind, though, and unfortunately she slipped on an icy patch, bringing Pat down and landing heavily on top of her. Scrambling to her feet, Morag trampled on Pat's hand and the girl yelped with pain.

Miss Wilton blew her whistle furiously, while several of the girls rushed across to Pat, who was sitting on the ground, nursing her injured hand and biting her lip in pain.

'Are you OK, Pat?' asked Isabel anxiously, before whirling round on Morag. 'You did that on purpose!'

'I didn't!' shouted the girl indignantly. 'I slipped on a patch of ice and . . .'

'Go and get changed, Morag,' ordered the games teacher sternly. 'I'll speak to you later.'

Angrily, the girl marched off the court blinking back hot tears, determined that the others wouldn't see them. It was so unfair! Games was the only thing she looked forward to, and now even that had been ruined. She really hadn't meant to hurt Pat, but it was no use telling that to the sixth form. They seemed determined to think the worst of her.

'I think you'd better take yourself off to Matron,' said Miss Wilton, looking at Pat's hand. 'Best to be on the safe side.'

So Pat went off to sickbay, knocking on the door with her uninjured hand.

'Come in!' called out Matron. 'Ah, Pat, I was just about to come looking for you. Good Heavens, whatever has happened to your hand?'

Pat told her and Matron examined the injury with gentle skill.

'No bones broken, but you'll have some beautiful bruises tomorrow,' she said briskly. 'Lucky it's your left hand. Morag's a fierce one, all right.'

Pat agreed but, now that her pain was beginning to subside and she knew that no serious damage was done, her natural sense of fair play came to the fore. 'I honestly believe it was an accident, Matron,' she said. 'The ground was pretty slippery in places because of all the frost we've had.'

'It's good of you to take it like that, but whether you'll feel so generous towards Morag after you've heard what I have to say is another matter.'

'What do you mean, Matron?' asked Pat, frowning.

'Well, if you remember, I said that I was just about to go looking for you when you came in?'

Pat nodded.

'The reason being that I had just done a spot-check on the sixth's dormitories and I'm afraid yours fell way below standard, Pat.'

'But all of the girls in my dormitory are sticklers for making their beds and keeping their things tidy,' said Pat in dismay. 'They wouldn't dare be anything else with you as Matron!'

'*Most* of them are sticklers, I agree,' said Matron meaningfully. 'But there's one girl in your form who's let the side down. Morag left her bed in a disgraceful state this morning: unmade, clothes strewn across it, and goodness knows what else. You know what that means, don't you, Pat?'

Pat's lips tightened grimly. She knew all right. An order mark! Order marks were given for misbehaviour or breaking rules and, if too many were earned, resulted in loss of privileges for the whole form. Among the lower school a few order marks weren't regarded as a very serious matter. The upper school, however, considered them a great disgrace. In fact, Pat couldn't remember any sixth form ever having an order mark against it since she had been at St Clare's. Just wait until she got hold of Morag!

'If such a thing had happened in the first or second form I would have given the girl responsible a good telling off and, perhaps, a second chance,' said Matron. 'Unfortunately I can't do that with a sixth former. At your age you're all expected to know better.'

'Yes, Matron,' agreed Pat, outwardly calm while inside she was seething. 'I'll have a word with Morag.'

'I don't doubt it, Pat,' Matron said with dry amusement at the head girl's grim expression. 'Two or three words, if I'm any judge of the matter. Don't lose your temper too badly and put yourself in the wrong, though, will you?'

'I won't,' promised Pat as she left Matron's room. Inwardly she didn't feel quite so sure.

Pat made her way down to the changing-rooms and there was the Scottish girl, sitting on a bench and changing her shoes.

'Pat,' she said, flushing as the head girl entered. 'I'm sorry about your hand. I really didn't mean . . .'

'Never mind that,' interrupted Pat, brushing the apology aside. 'Morag, why didn't you make your bed this morning?'

In a flash the girl's apologetic demeanour changed to one of stubborn anger as she snapped, 'Is that why you're here? To tell me off as though I were a first former? Well, don't waste your time, Pat, because I won't have it.' With that she got up and stalked to the door, but Pat was too quick for her. Darting in front of Morag, she slammed the door so hard that it echoed.

'Let me pass,' demanded Morag through gritted teeth as the other girl leant against the door.

'No,' said Pat, quite furious now. 'Not until you've heard me out. Thanks to you, we now have the distinction of being the only sixth form in the history of St Clare's to have an order mark against us! Can't you see that we're all sick to death of your stupid ways? It's time you grew up! You're a disgrace to the school and your parents.'

'How dare you?' gasped Morag, turning a little pale.

'I dare because I'm head girl and I care a great deal about the reputation of the sixth and the honour of St Clare's.'

Morag sneered. 'Well, I don't!'

'Tell me something I don't know!' said Pat in disgust. 'I can understand why your folks wanted to send you to boarding school, but not why Miss Theobald agreed to accept you. You've nothing to gain from your time here, because you've nothing to offer in return. Your work isn't up to first-form standard, while your behaviour belongs in the kindergarten. Well, Morag, just carry on as you are and, with a bit of luck, you'll be expelled. Your mum and dad will be upset, but I don't suppose you care for them any more than you do for anything else. One thing's for sure – the sixth won't be sorry to see the back of you.'

Morag trembled from head to foot as she listened to this scornful speech, wanting to stop the stream of angry, contemptuous words that poured from Pat's lips. But just then Pat was forced to move aside as someone pushed the door from the other side, and Carlotta entered.

'How are your fingers, Pat?' she began, then stopped, realizing that the atmosphere was tense and seeing the stormy expressions on both girls' faces. Then Morag brushed past her and walked away.

'What goes on?' asked Carlotta in astonishment. 'Have you and Morag been rowing about the way she tackled you? You look ready to explode.'

'I already have,' said Pat, and told the girl about Morag's order mark. Some of the other sixth formers came in as she was speaking, and were furious.

'What a total idiot she is!'

'It's so unfair when the rest of us take the trouble to make sure the dormitories are tidy.'

'Send her to Coventry!'

Hilary wrinkled her nose thoughtfully at this last cry. 'In Morag's case, I don't think it would make much difference,' she said. 'Because she doesn't want our company anyway.'

'Well, something's got to be done,' said Anne-Marie. 'We can't have her chalking up any more order marks for the sixth.'

The others agreed. But what?

'I feel as though I'm partly to blame,' said Carlotta

gravely. 'Miss Theobald asked me to befriend her and I've failed miserably.'

There were cries of protest at this.

'It's certainly not your fault!' said Janet. 'She's impossible, and the head will soon come to realize that, just as the other mistresses have. With a bit of luck, Morag might even be sent down into the fifth form.'

Carlotta looked sharply at Janet and said thoughtfully, 'Yes, she might. Thanks, Janet, you've just given me an idea.'

In their study that evening, Morag and Carlotta sat either side of the table, working silently at their French prep. Glancing briefly across at the other girl's book, Carlotta could see that she had covered only a few lines with her sprawling, untidy writing. And half of that had been crossed out! Looking back at her own page of neatly written work, she bit back a grin. Mam'zelle would hit the roof if Morag handed that in tomorrow. But the Scottish girl didn't seem to care, laying down her pen and pushing the book away from her with a sigh.

'Someone must have forgotten to tell Mam'zelle that we're meant to be taking it easy this term,' remarked Carlotta. 'She always gives us twice as much prep as the other mistresses. Still, you won't have to worry about it for much longer. The work's a breeze down in the fifth.'

Morag frowned. 'What do you mean?'

'Oh, only that I happened to overhear Miss Harry and the head talking together this morning, and they said . . .' Carlotta's voice trailed off and she put a hand up to her mouth. 'Oops! Maybe I shouldn't have said anything, but I assumed that Miss Harry had already spoken to you about it.'

'Spoken about what? What are you talking about?' demanded Morag impatiently.

'Well, Miss Harry told the head that your work and conduct weren't really up to the standard of the sixth,' said Carlotta innocently. 'Miss Theobald agreed that if there was no improvement over the next couple of weeks, you were to go down into the fifth.' Wicked Carlotta crossed her fingers behind her back as she said all of this, hoping that the unpredictable Morag wouldn't storm off to the head to demand the truth. She didn't, instead she looked rather pale and stricken as she said hoarsely, 'But the head can't do that!'

Carlotta raised her dark brows. 'Miss Theobald can do anything she chooses. It's quite usual, you know, for a girl to be put back a year if she can't – or won't – keep up with her class.'

Then, seeing how appalled Morag looked, she added kindly, 'You might feel more at home in the fifth. They're a good crowd and not quite so mature and responsible as our lot. Anyway, look on the bright side – you'll have a whole extra year in which to enjoy St Clare's.'

For a moment, Morag suspected Carlotta of laughing at her, but the girl had bent her head to her work again, looking the picture of innocence as she scribbled away. How she was laughing inside, though, at Morag's horror.

And, indeed, the girl *was* horrified. She had meant to be so unhappy and badly behaved that her father would take her away at half-term. Instead it seemed that she might have to endure an extra year in this rotten place! Well, she wasn't standing for that! If her only chance of getting out of it was by changing her ways and proving that she could keep up with the others, that was what she would have to do. Taking up her pen, she applied herself once more to her French book. Mam'zelle would be pleasantly surprised in tomorrow's class.

Carlotta watched her through lowered lashes, noting the changing expressions on the girl's striking face. Lying went right against her nature but, on this occasion, the girl felt that it had been justified. Certainly it seemed to have worked, Morag's pen was flying across the page. Carlotta felt encouraged. Next weekend, she decided, once the Thursday meeting was out of the way, she would make a real effort to get to know Morag better.

9

The first meeting

'I can't tell you how much I envy you,' said Mirabel to Gladys as she called into her study on Thursday evening. 'The first meeting tonight and I'll miss it! Gladys, why was I such a pig-headed idiot last term?'

'No use thinking like that,' said Gladys giving her friend a clap on the shoulder. 'You have to look forward and think what fun you'll be able to have after you've passed the exams. And you *will* pass this time, Mirabel, I know it.'

'Thanks, Gladys,' said Mirabel gruffly, flushing a little as she always did at any show of affection. 'Well, if hard work has anything to do with it, I certainly ought to pass, because I've spent every spare minute studying. So has Angela.'

'Really?' said Gladys, surprised. 'I must say, I didn't think she had it in her to work hard.'

'Oh, she can work when she wants something badly enough,' said Mirabel with a touch of scorn. 'And she's determined to get to this fancy finishing school of hers at all costs.' The girl grinned suddenly. 'Although knowing that Carlotta will be going with her has taken the edge off it a little.'

'I wouldn't be too sure about that,' said Gladys drily. 'Carlotta wants to get *out* of going every bit as badly as Angela wants to get in. And Miss Theobald has promised to have a few words with her father on the subject.'

'Great news!' cried Mirabel, pleased. 'I won't tell Angela, though. It'll do her good to think she's not going to have everything all her own way for once.'

'How are the two of you getting on?'

Mirabel wrinkled her brow. 'Well, we both spend so much time with our noses in books that there isn't much conversation. But, in a way, it's created a kind of bond between us. All the same, I'll be glad when the exams are over. How about you and Alison?'

'Oh, Alison's OK. We don't always share the same ideas, but she's kind and good natured.' She laughed. 'A little *too* good natured at times! The first former who comes to do our jobs has become very attached to her. Poor Alison's getting really bored with the way she hangs round, but can't bring herself to hurt the kid's feelings.'

Right on cue there came a soft tapping at the door, and Joan Terry put her head in. The soft brown eyes dimmed a little as she realized that Alison wasn't there. 'Hi, Gladys!' she said. 'Where's Alison?'

'Gone to see Angela,' answered Gladys. 'But what do you want her for, Joan? You came in earlier to do everything that needed doing.'

'Yes, but I was bored in our common-room,' said the girl hesitantly. 'I thought that maybe there was something else I could do for Alison.'

Gladys frowned. Although she had joked about Joan's devotion with Mirabel, something wasn't quite right here. The girl ought to be making friends in her own form and joining in the many lively activities there, instead of constantly trotting after a sixth former like a little dog. Fortunately, Alison wasn't the kind of person to take advantage of Joan's slavish loyalty, but Gladys still felt uneasy. She tried to give the girl's thoughts another direction. 'You did a great job in goal the other day, Joan. Keep up the practice, because I need all the promising players I can get.'

'You bet I will,' said Joan, flushing with pleasure. 'Will you tell Alison that I came by? And that I'll be here tomorrow at my usual time.'

'Yes, I'll tell her. Now you'd better get back to your common-room.'

Joan went and Mirabel said generously, 'You really are doing brilliantly as games captain. I haven't had much time to come and watch the young ones myself, but I'd have to be deaf not to hear the way the lower school sing your praises.'

Gladys certainly had a way with the younger girls, warmly praising those who were good and gently encouraging those who were less able. Like Mirabel, she had the gift of inspiring the girls with wanting to do their best for her. Unlike Mirabel, it hadn't gone to her head. Gladys admired her friend for being able to praise her so wholeheartedly, without a trace of bitterness, and said with her usual modesty, 'Bobby and Janet are a great help. They often spot things that I might have missed. It was Janet who thought of trying out Joan in goal. Oh, just look at the time! I'd better shoot off to the common-room or I'll be late for the first meeting. Don't feel too left out, Mirabel. I'll come and tell you all about it as soon as I have time.'

The others were already in the common-room when Gladys arrived, seated around the big table. Gladys slipped in beside Claudine and looked around. There was Priscilla, sitting up very straight and looking strangely excited for once. No doubt delighted at the prospect of sticking her nose into other people's business, thought Gladys. Beyond her sat Morag, looking rather subdued. The girls had noticed a change in the Scottish girl over the last couple of days. She actually seemed to have settled down a bit and, although she was still surly with the sixth formers, her behaviour in class had improved greatly, as had her work.

'Well, here we all are,' said Doris. 'But what do we do now?'

'Just wait until someone knocks at the door,' said Isabel. 'And hope that it won't be too long.'

'Suppose no one comes?' said Anne-Marie. 'Maybe no one has any worries or problems this week.'

'In a school of this size there's *always* someone who needs to get something off their chest,' said Hilary sagely. 'They'll come all right.'

And so they did, in a steady stream. First was a dark

girl called Hilda, who complained that her best friend was always copying her work.

'Haven't the teachers caught on?' asked Bobby. 'They must be getting suspicious if you both keep handing in identical assignments.'

'Oh, Ruth doesn't copy it word for word – just pinches my ideas! Last Saturday, for example, we were supposed to be working on a joint project. Then Ruth decided to go off roller-skating with the others and left me to do all the work. But she still took half the credit.'

'OK, Hilda,' said Pat kindly. 'You go and wait outside while we talk it through, and we'll call you back when we come up with a solution.'

This procedure had been agreed on beforehand by the girls. 'So that if we have differing ideas on how to settle a problem we can thrash it out in private,' Isabel had said. 'It's not going to look too good if we start arguing in front of the kids.'

'It's not on,' said Fizz indignantly now. 'Hilda needs to tell Ruth where to get off.'

'Yes, but not everyone's quite as blunt as you are, Fizz,' said Hilary with a smile. 'Ruth's a bit full of herself, whereas Hilda's on the shy side and not too good at sticking up for herself.'

'Ruth's cheating,' declared Priscilla pompously. 'If you ask me, she ought to be reported to Miss Roberts.'

'Trust you to come up with a solution like that!' said Bobby scornfully. The girl flushed angrily and debated whether to say something cutting in return. Then she caught the challenging look in Bobby's eye and hastily changed her mind. Anyone who engaged in a verbal battle with sharp-witted Bobby generally came second.

'I think Hilda ought to speak to her about it,' said Isabel decidedly. 'But in her own time. It won't be easy for her, but if she knows she has our support, she just might be able to work up to it. Agreed?'

There was a chorus of assent, with the exception of Priscilla, who said, 'I still think . . .'

'Well, you're out-voted, so just shut up,' said Bobby rudely. 'Great idea, Isabel. And it'll do wonders for Hilda's self-confidence if she can make a stand.'

'Shall I fetch her back?' asked Fizz. Isabel nodded and Hilda was brought back into the room. She listened intently as Isabel spoke, saying at last, 'I know you're right. I guess I've always been a bit afraid of standing up to Ruth because I don't want to lose her as a friend. She's the leader, you see, while I just sort of tag along. She's so popular while I don't find it so easy to make friends.'

'If she's any kind of a friend this shouldn't make a difference,' Fizz remarked. 'And if it does . . . well, you're better off without her.'

'Absolutely right,' agreed Pat. 'OK, Hilda, you just think about what we've said and come back in a few weeks to let us know how you're doing.'

'Well, I don't think we handled that too badly, if I do say so myself,' said Janet. 'It's great that we can reach agreement so smoothly – or at least, most of us can.' On these words she looked directly at Priscilla, who suddenly seemed to find the table fascinating, refusing to meet Janet's steady gaze. Then a timid knock sounded on the door. It opened slightly and a head appeared.

'Come in,' called Pat. 'We don't bite.'

A small figure sidled in, shaking so badly that the girls could almost hear her knees knocking.

'Lucy, isn't it?' said Pat pleasantly. 'Well, take a seat and tell us what we can do for you.'

Lucy sat, feeling very small and insignificant. Haltingly she brought out her story. 'Last week it was my friend Susan's birthday,' she began shyly. 'I'd been planning to buy her something special, because when it was my birthday she bought me a record and took me out for tea. But this month my folks were late sending me my allowance, so I was broke.'

'Don't tell me the two of you have fallen out just because you didn't get her a present?' said Gladys.

'No,' answered Lucy. 'Because as it turned out, I was able to buy her something at the last minute.'

'How come?' asked Doris. 'Did you borrow from someone?'

Lucy gulped. 'No . . . I found a ten-pound-note in the corridor and picked it up.'

'You should have handed it in to Matron immediately,' said Priscilla sharply, drawing glares from the rest of the sixth form.

'I know,' said Lucy miserably. 'And I honestly meant to. But I suddenly thought how pleased Susan would be if, for her birthday, I could buy her the bag she's had her eye on. So that's what I did. And then something awful happened!'

'What?' asked Bobby curiously.

'Well, Susan told me that she had lost the ten-pound-note her older brother had sent her as a present. Which means that *I* must have picked it up! I know that I should have told her right away but, somehow, the longer I left it, the harder it became.' Tears started in Lucy's eyes. 'I'm in such a mess, and I don't know what to do.'

Kind-hearted Alison came round the table and put her arm round the girl's heaving shoulders. 'Don't worry, Lucy,' she said, almost on the verge of tears herself. 'What you've done isn't so very bad.' She looked around the table for support and Pat said at once, 'Of course not. Just one of those spur of the moment things. Go with Alison, Lucy, while we sort it out. And don't look so upset. You haven't robbed a bank, you know.'

Lucy gave a laugh, mingled with a sob which turned into a hiccup, and allowed Alison to lead her from the room.

'Poor kid,' said Anne-Marie. 'She's obviously been worrying herself sick over this. 'Priscilla, did you have to be so sharp with her?'

'What she did was wrong,' said Priscilla piously. 'I think she should be made to tell the truth at once, otherwise it could lead to all kinds of things.'

'Don't be so stupid!' said Janet impatiently. 'It's

obvious that Lucy isn't dishonest, or she wouldn't have worked herself up into such a state.'

'Yes,' agreed Doris. 'It's the sort of thing anyone in her position might have done on the spur of the moment, and regretted later.'

Alison returned then, saying, 'She's calmed down a bit now. Any ideas, girls?'

'I think Lucy ought to tell the truth,' put in Carlotta unexpectedly. 'But not until she's saved up enough money to pay Susan back. Then she'll know Lucy's really sorry. With a bit of luck they might even be able to laugh about it.'

'Yes, and it would definitely ease Lucy's mind if she owned up,' said Pat. 'Fetch her back, would you, Alison?'

Lucy's eyes were still red when she returned, but she clearly felt a little happier for having shared her guilty secret.

'We really think that you ought to own up to Susan,' said Pat. 'But after you've saved up enough money to pay her back. If she is mad with you and the two of you fall out over it, then come back to us and we'll try to put it right for you. Personally, though, I don't think you've much to worry about.'

'Yes, I think I knew all along that owning up was the right thing to do,' Lucy said. 'I just needed some-one to give me a little push. I should be able to pay her back next month – and won't it be a weight off my shoulders.'

'Phew!' said Hilary as the door closed behind the girl.

'I'm absolutely exhausted. Who would have thought that being an agony aunt could be so tiring?'

'It's not over yet,' said Isabel as someone knocked at the door. 'Next, please!'

A ride - and a revelation

Saturday morning dawned bright and clear, the sun shining although there was a chill in the air.

A perfect day for riding, thought Carlotta, who was a regular at the stables along the road, swiftly pulling on jodhpurs and a sweater before setting off. To her surprise, she found Morag there, watching as Will, the owner's son, tacked up a frisky grey mare.

'Hi, Carlotta!' he said, looking up and giving a friendly grin. 'With you in a sec.'

'No hurry, Will,' she replied with an answering smile, before turning to the Scottish girl. 'I didn't know you rode, Morag. Mind if I tag along?'

'Suit yourself,' replied the girl with a shrug. 'But I aim to go for a good, long gallop. I'm an experienced rider and if you can't keep up with me, I'll leave you behind.'

Will, who had struck up quite a friendship with Carlotta, stared narrowly at Morag and opened his mouth to say something. Then Carlotta caught his eye and winked, shaking her head. To Morag she said meekly, 'I'll try not to slow you down.'

'It's obvious your pal's never seen you in action,' murmured Will as the Scottish girl mounted her horse and he led out a handsome chestnut for Carlotta. 'I reckon you'll leave her standing.'

'She's not my pal, Will,' answered Carlotta ruefully. 'Not yet, anyhow. Don't bother with a saddle for me – mustn't keep Morag waiting.' With that she grabbed the horse's mane and, with the agility of an acrobat, vaulted lightly on to his back. 'Come on, Morag,' she called brightly. 'I'll race you to that big oak tree over there.'

Leaving Will to stare after them, the two girls trotted out of the yard, their horses picking up speed as they came into an open field, faster and faster, breaking into a canter, then a gallop. The cold air stung the girls' cheeks, bringing a rosy glow to them and an excited sparkle to their eyes. Carlotta won the race by a head and had her reward when Morag called out in admiration, 'You can certainly ride, Carlotta!'

'I was practically born on horseback,' answered the girl. 'Anyway, you weren't exactly holding back yourself.'

For the first time since she had come to St Clare's, Morag grinned and Carlotta was amazed at how different she looked, so pretty and friendly. 'Do you have a horse at home?'

'Yes, he's called Starlight,' answered Morag. 'And I miss him so much.' Then, as though afraid of revealing too much of herself, she clammed up again and trotted away.

Oh, no! thought Carlotta. Just as I was making progress. She decided to give Morag a surprise. Balancing herself very carefully, she stood on the horse's broad back. Then, with a soft chirruping noise, she coaxed him forward, catching up with Morag.

'Fancy another race?' she asked. Morag turned her head, giving a gasp of surprise as she found herself staring at Carlotta's legs where she had expected her face to be.

'Carlotta, you're mad!' she cried. 'Get down before you fall.'

'If you insist,' said Carlotta wickedly. Then, to Morag's amazement, she sprang from the horse's back, landing in side-saddle position.

'You *are* mad!' said Morag, beginning to laugh in spite of herself. 'Totally loopy, in fact!'

'I am once I get on horseback,' agreed Carlotta happily. 'There are some jumps in the paddock over there. Let's go and show one another what we can do.'

So it came about that Carlotta spent a more pleasant day than she would have believed possible with Morag, both girls showing off shamelessly and praising one another extravagantly.

'I haven't had such a good time in ages,' said Morag as the girls made their way back to school.

'It was great!' agreed Carlotta. 'We ought to make it a regular thing.'

As the day was so fine, some of the sixth formers had challenged the fifth to a friendly game of netball. They were just about to begin when Morag and Carlotta, positively glowing from their morning in the fresh air, returned to St Clare's. Pat, happening to glance round, was struck by how different Morag looked – almost happy. Perhaps now would be a good time to make amends for the harsh words she had spoken to the girl the other day. After all, Morag did seem to be making a little more effort now. Smiling, Pat walked across to the two girls and said in her friendly manner, 'Enjoyed your ride? How about joining us for netball if you're not too tired out, Carlotta? We're a player short. Morag, if you're at a loose end we could do with an umpire too.'

But, to both Pat and Carlotta's dismay, Morag's face resumed its habitual glower and she walked off without a word.

'Aargh!' cried Carlotta, clutching at her hair. 'Just as I was beginning to get through to her.'

'My fault,' said Pat ruefully. 'Evidently the only place Morag wants to bury the hatchet is in my head! She has improved in class, though – your doing?'

Carlotta grinned. 'I may have had something to do with it. I told her that the head was thinking of sending her down into the fifth and the thought of spending another year here had a strange effect on her.'

'Carlotta, you're wicked,' said Pat in mock horror. 'Still, it seems to have done the trick.'

'Hey, Pat! Carlotta!' called out Fizz. 'Come on, we're waiting to start!'

'Count me out, Pat,' said Carlotta, a sudden determined look coming over her face. 'I'm going to try and sort things out with Morag once and for all.'

'Best of luck,' said Pat, not looking very hopeful. 'All right, Fizz. Keep your hair on – I'm coming!'

Morag was cleaning her riding boots when Carlotta entered the study and said, 'You should get one of the first formers to do that.'

'I'm quite capable of doing things for myself,' replied Morag abruptly. 'I think it's a stupid, outdated custom anyway.'

Carlotta raised her eyebrows. 'It teaches the younger girls to be responsible and they get their turn at giving out orders when they reach the upper school.'

'I can do without the lecture, thanks,' retorted Morag, her green eyes icy.

'I wasn't lecturing,' said Carlotta, holding tightly on to her own temper. 'Morag, why were you so rude to Pat just then?'

'I don't like her, or they way she thinks that being head girl gives her the right to speak to me as if I was about five years old. I'm used to doing as I please.'

'Maybe, but can you imagine what St Clare's would be like if all of us went around doing and saying what we pleased?' asked Carlotta. 'And it *is* Pat's duty to see that the rules are kept.'

'I thought you weren't going to lecture me,' said Morag sullenly.

'I just wish that you'd give Pat and the rest of us a chance,' Carlotta persisted. 'If you'd just be sensible and try to join in you might . . .'

'I don't *want* to join in,' broke in Morag angrily. 'I'm not like you, or Pat, or any of the others, can't you see that? It's all right for you – you've been here for years and were brought up to this kind of life. Well, I wasn't and I hate it.' With that she slammed out of the room. Trembling with anger herself, Carlotta resisted the temptation to go after her and tell her exactly what she thought of her. Then, as suddenly as it had risen, her anger vanished and, sighing, she sank down into an armchair. She had failed! Miss Theobald had been wrong to entrust her with such a delicate task. The calm, tactful Hilary would have been a much better choice. On Monday she would go to the head and tell her so. In the meantime it was of no use to sit here brooding. She may as well join the others at netball and work off some of her temper.

Morag, meanwhile, made her way to the common-room, hoping that it would be empty. She badly needed to be alone with her thoughts. This morning she had been able to put her troubles right out of her mind in her exhilaration at being on horseback and – she had to admit – her pleasure in Carlotta's company. For a short while their mutual love of horses had created a bond between the two girls. But it had been a fragile bond, broken now. Miserably, the girl peeped round the door, pulling a face as she saw Alison and Claudine, neither of whom cared for fresh air, curled up cosily on armchairs near the fire. Morag moved away, the two girls in the room unaware of her presence as they chatted amicably. Then Claudine said something in her clear voice that made the girl pause. She knew it was wrong to eavesdrop, but Morag stood rooted to the spot, listening.

And what she heard was to help change her view of St Clare's for ever.

Carlotta felt hungry and pleasantly tired after the boisterous, good-natured netball game. Thank goodness it was Saturday and there was no prep. If it wasn't for her study-mate, she would be looking forward to tea, followed by a nice, lazy evening doing nothing. Oh, well, she supposed she could always go down to the dining-room for school tea. But when Carlotta popped into the study to change her shoes, she was happily surprised. A fresh, white cloth had been placed over the table, laid for two, and on it stood an array of sandwiches, crisps and a huge, squidgy chocolate cake.

'Oh, good, you're back.' Morag turned from the window with a hesitant smile. Gesturing towards the table she said, 'Sit down and help yourself. I thought you'd be hungry after a day spent outdoors.'

Recognising this as an olive-branch, Carlotta smiled back and said, 'I'm starving. And this looks – well, good enough to eat. It must have taken you ages to get this lot ready.'

'Oh, I got Susan from the first form to help me,' said Morag, flushing a little as she sat down. 'Tea OK? Or there's ginger beer if you'd prefer?'

'Tea's fine.' Carlotta watched Morag narrowly. Something had happened to change her mind – the question was, what?

There was silence for a few minutes as the two girls ate hungrily, then Morag cleared her throat and began,

'Look, Carlotta, I'm sorry about what I said earlier. I didn't realize that you . . .'

She broke off and Carlotta said sharply, 'Didn't realize that I what?'

Morag sighed. 'Well, the thing is, after I flounced out of here like an idiot, I went along to the common-room and heard two of the girls talking. Your name was mentioned and I listened.' She bit her lip. 'I know it was wrong of me, but I'm glad now that I did, because I learnt something. You see, I heard them saying that you had once belonged to a circus, and how you had loved the life there. Then I heard how difficult it had been for you to adapt to a completely different way of life here. But you stuck at it because you wanted to please your dad and make him proud of you.'

Carlotta nodded, her puzzled frown clearing as it dawned on her why Morag had undergone such a drastic change. The girl was so used to everyone in the school knowing about her unusual past that it simply hadn't occurred to her that to Morag it would be news. If only she had told the new girl all about herself from the start, how much easier things might have been!

'Will you tell me about your life in the circus?' asked Morag rather shyly. 'And about how you managed to settle down here?'

So Carlotta talked about her circus days, rather wistfully at times, of the people she had lived with and of how her father had come looking for her when her mother had died. Morag listened raptly. 'I should have guessed, when you performed those crazy tricks today!' she exclaimed. 'Tell me more.'

But Carlotta shook her head. 'I've talked about myself enough. I'd rather hear about Morag Stuart, and why she's so determined to be awkward and bad tempered when, deep down, she's quite nice!'

Morag blushed in earnest this time. She looked rather pensive for a moment then began, 'My mum died when I was a baby, so I was brought up by Dad. We lived in a big, rambling house in the most beautiful Scottish glen you could imagine and it was a wonderful life. I was allowed to run wild most of the time and my days were spent riding, swimming in the loch and fishing.'

'I see. But didn't you go to school?' asked Carlotta.

'I went to the village school sometimes. Dad's a writer, you see, and works from home, so we used to have what he called "bunking off" days together. Quite a lot of bunking off days! We'd just take off on horse-back and go fishing, or for a picnic. Carlotta, it was the best life anyone could wish for.'

No wonder Morag couldn't settle, thought Carlotta. St Clare's must seem like a prison to her after that kind of life. But what had made her dad suddenly decide to send her away?

'Then Marian arrived,' explained the girl, as though she'd read Carlotta's mind. 'She came to our village to stay with relatives and Dad met her at a dinner party. Suddenly our bunking off days were over, and he was spending every spare minute with her. And before I knew what had happened, they were married.'

And Morag, having had her father to herself all her life, had resented it bitterly, Carlotta guessed. So it seemed, as Morag poured out the rest of her tale.

'She disapproved terribly of me, and the way Dad had brought me up. And she thought I spent too much time with Starlight and not enough on my school work.' Morag paused, turning a little red. 'It wasn't all her fault, though. I went out of my way to be rude and make life difficult for her. In the end, the house just wasn't big enough for the two of us, so here I am.'

Carlotta eyed her thoughtfully for while, then said, 'No wonder you're so fed up here. But I reckon your dad's to blame as well. If he'd included you in his plans and let you get to know Marian before they married, instead of pushing you out, perhaps you wouldn't have felt so hostile towards her. But I think that you ought to be pleased for your dad. I know I'd be delighted if mine found someone who could make him happy.'

'I never thought of it that way,' said Morag slowly. 'Too wrapped up in myself, I suppose.'

'Yes, you have been,' said Carlotta in her forthright way. 'But I think your stepmother might have done you a favour by insisting you come here.'

'Oh?' Morag looked extremely doubtful.

'Well, how can you know what you really want from life if you don't experience different things?' said Carlotta, sounding very mature and wise to the confused girl at that moment. 'When you leave St

Clare's you may decide to return to your beautiful Scottish glen. Or you may choose to do something quite different, like train for a career or go to college. The point is, if you hadn't left home then your view of the world and your choices would have been far narrower.'

'You're right,' said Morag, things seeming to fall into place. 'I've been a bit of an idiot, haven't I? But I won't be again, believe me.'

Carlotta did.

'Will you promise me something, Carlotta?' asked the Scottish girl, looking solemn.

'Anything,' agreed Carlotta, already liking this new Morag.

'If you see me slipping back into my old, stupid, sullen ways, kick me – good and hard.'

'I will,' Carlotta laughed. 'Although somehow I don't think I'll need to. Now, did you say something about ginger beer? All this straight talking has given me a thirst!'

11

Priscilla stirs things up

Mischief was brewing in the first-form common-room. The Lacey twins, their long punishment now behind them, were finding the strain of trying to be good too much and were in the mood for excitement.

'I feel a trick coming on,' announced Dora. 'Possibly in maths tomorrow.'

Katie turned down the corners of her mouth and shook her head.

'Oh, Katie! Don't say you're going to be a wet blanket about playing tricks just because you're head of the form?' Dora pleaded.

'Not at all,' answered Katie. 'But everyone knows Mam'zelle is the best person to play tricks on. You'll never manage to put one over on Miss Roberts – she's too sharp.'

'*You* might not,' said Dora haughtily. 'But *I* would. I just love a challenge, isn't that right, Daphne?'

Her twin nodded absent-mindedly. 'Mm. But if you ask me, a midnight party's a better way to relieve boredom.'

This suggestion found instant favour, a dozen or more voices chorusing, 'Brilliant! Let's do it!'

'Well, it is a kind of tradition, I suppose,' said Katie.

'Anyone got a birthday coming up?'

'Mine's in a fortnight,' said a girl called Rita. 'My folks usually send me money, and I don't mind putting some of it towards a party.'

'Great!' cried Daphne. 'So, if the rest of us buy some food as well, we can celebrate Rita's birthday in style.'

Joan Terry was not present at this meeting, being busy in Alison's study. Her jobs finished, she made her way back to the common-room and had just turned a corner when she gave a sudden gasp. There outside the door, nose practically in the keyhole, stood Priscilla. She tried to draw back, but her gasp had given her away and Priscilla turned sharply, her mean eyes narrowing. Joan was shocked, for although she knew that the sixth former had a reputation for snooping, to catch her in the act like this was just awful. Worse still, the girl could do nothing about it. If she told the first formers, or put them on their guard in any way, Priscilla would pay her back in the cruellest way possible.

Silently Priscilla beckoned Joan forward and, as she reached Priscilla's side, she heard Katie's voice saying quite clearly, 'A midnight party it is, then. We've two weeks to organize everything, so that should give us plenty of time.'

Joan's hand flew to her mouth in horror as she saw Priscilla's thin lips stretch into a queerly triumphant smile and, bravely, she stepped forward, placing her hand on the doorknob. She had to stop the first form giving anything else away. But her action came too late, for at that moment the door swung away from her, opened from the inside, and Rita stood there, the colour leaving her face as she saw who Joan was with. Poor Joan was very flustered and showed it, but Priscilla carried off the situation in her usual arrogant manner, walking calmly into the common-room and turning off the radio. The first formers felt uncomfortable, yet angry as well. Not one of the other sixth formers would have dreamt of invading the younger girls' privacy in such a way.

'Girls,' began Priscilla in a silky tone that they mistrusted at once. 'I'm looking for a volunteer to do a little work for me.' She looked round the room, but none of the girls would meet her gaze. Her eyes snapped coldly and she said angrily, 'Well, I don't think I've ever met such a set of rude, unhelpful kids! When I was your age, if a senior girl snapped her fingers we jumped, and . . .'

'Pity you didn't jump in the river,' muttered Daphne under her breath.

Priscilla's sharp ears caught the remark and she rounded on the girl, demanding, 'What did you say?'

Daphne, unabashed, stared at Priscilla, obviously quite ready to repeat her remark. But as she opened her mouth, Joan, shaking in her shoes and unable to bear the tension a moment longer, said nervously, 'I'll do your jobs for you, Priscilla.'

Every head turned in her direction and the girl wished that the ground would open up as she read the others' scornful thoughts. Coward! Traitor! Much to her surprise, Priscilla declined her offer, patting her shoulder and saying in a smooth voice, 'Thank you, Joan. It's nice to know that *one* member of the first form is willing to help. But you've already been working hard for Alison and I couldn't possibly expect you to do my jobs as well. Susan!' She picked on the girl whose ten-pound-note Lucy had mistakenly picked up. 'And you, Ruth.' This was the first former Hilda had complained of. 'You two will do. Come on.'

Reluctantly, pulling faces at Priscilla behind her back that made the others want to giggle, the two first formers followed her from the room. Once the door was closed behind them, the twins rounded on Joan.

'I'll do your jobs for you, Priscilla,' mimicked Dora cruelly. 'And can I lick your boots clean for you?'

'Yes, and what were you doing listening outside the door with her?' demanded Rita, pushing Joan roughly in the shoulder. 'Just what did you hear, you little snitch?'

'Nothing!' said Joan, almost in tears. 'I wasn't listening. Honestly I wasn't.'

'I'll bet that sneak Priscilla was, though,' said Daphne. 'And it wouldn't surprise me if you were covering up for her. Well, she'd better not get to know any first-form secrets, that's all. Because if she does, we'll know who told her.'

But, of course, Priscilla already knew some of the first form's secrets. Things that she hadn't learnt from Joan or from listening outside doors, but that she had discovered from the Thursday meeting. And the girl meant to use them to stir up trouble for the two first formers who were helping tidy her study – although this was so neat that there was hardly anything for them to do and they began to wonder why Priscilla wanted them there. They soon found out.

'I hear you lost ten pounds last week, Susan,' she said. 'Rather careless of you.'

Susan flushed. 'I didn't realize there was a hole in my pocket,' she said shortly. 'But how did you get to hear about it?'

'Oh, Lucy told me about it, after she found it,' said Priscilla innocently.

'But Lucy didn't find it!' said Susan, her eyes sparkling angrily. 'She's my friend and she'd have handed it back to me straight away.'

'If you're so sure why don't you ask her?' suggested Priscilla, with a smug smile.

'I will,' retorted Susan. 'And you'll be proved wrong, you'll see.' But inwardly the girl felt uneasy. It seemed impossible that her friend could have done something so low, yet Priscilla sounded sure.

'You'd be surprised how much I know about the goings-on in your form,' said Priscilla slyly. 'For example, I know all about your nasty little ways, Ruth.'

'Me?' said Ruth, startled. 'What have *I* done?'

'You cheat,' said Priscilla. 'And you make use of a girl who's supposed to be your friend.'

'I don't know what you're talking about!' cried Ruth, completely bewildered.

'No? The only reason you're friends with Hilda is because she gets good marks and you can copy her work, isn't it? And I happen to know that Hilda feels pretty sore about it, because she told me so herself.'

'That's not why I'm her friend at all!' gasped Ruth, turning pale. 'And if Hilda was mad at me, she'd say so to my face, not go behind my back – and to you, of all people!'

Priscilla flushed angrily. 'Just remember to show a little respect when you're speaking to your elders,' she snapped.

Respect, however, was the last thing either girl felt for Priscilla at that moment. Hurt and angry, they hurried over their tidying, anxious to get away from her spiteful accusations and get to the bottom of things.

'Hi, you two,' said Katie with a sympathetic grin when they got back to the common-room. 'Had a nice time with dear Priscilla?'

'We've had a most informative time,' replied Susan coldly as she spotted Lucy sitting in the corner. 'Hey, Lucy! I want a word with you.'

'Well, whatever's got into *her*?' asked Katie, astonished.

'A little bit of poison – courtesy of Priscilla,' answered Ruth grimly. 'Hilda, come here! You've got some explaining to do!'

After that, recriminations and accusations flew in all directions.

'I can't believe you would do something so low, Lucy,' burst out Susan. 'You *knew* I was upset about losing that money, and all the time *you* had it!'

'Hilda, I thought we were friends!' cried Ruth. 'Couldn't you have come and told me what was bothering you, instead of running to Priscilla? How you turn to *her*, of all people, beats me!'

'What's going on?' demanded Katie, pushing her way through the group that had gathered around the four girls – who looked as though they were about to have a free fight – and taking charge. Four angry voices spoke at once and Katie winced, holding up her hand for silence. 'One at a time! Lucy, you first.'

Stammering, her face red, Lucy told her story. A couple of the girls looked at her with contempt, but she was a well-liked girl and most of them felt for her, understanding that she had been sorely tempted. Even Susan calmed down and gave her friend a hug, saying warmly, 'I understand why you did it. Maybe I'd have done the same in your place. But next time you can't afford to buy me a present, just say so!'

Hilda spoke next and Ruth bit her lip. It was true, she realized in shame. She had used Hilda, never thinking how the girl felt about it. And poor Hilda had been afraid to confront her about it in case she lost her friendship. Suddenly Ruth felt about two feet tall. 'I'm sorry, Hilda,' she said humbly. 'I honestly thought you didn't mind me cribbing from you. You should have said. And it's not true that I'm friends with you just so that I can copy your work. We can *still* be friends, can't we?'

'You bet,' replied Hilda, her voice a little shaky.

'Thanks,' said Ruth. 'And if I ever ask to crib from you again, just tell me where to get off.'

'Well, I'm glad that's all been sorted out!' exclaimed Katie, wondering if there was a jinx on the first form today.

'There's one more thing to get sorted out,' put in Daphne. 'And that's the sixth form and their meetings. What's the point of us going to them with our personal problems if they're going to blab about them?'

'That's a bit unfair, Daphne,' protested Katie. 'It was only Priscilla who blabbed, with the intention of causing trouble. I'm sure that none of the other sixth formers would dream of breaking a confidence.'

'I agree,' said Rita. 'They're all really nice, apart from Priscilla. So what are we going to do about her?'

'Well, it's not really our place to do anything,' said Susan. 'It's up to the rest of the sixth to deal with her.'

'I don't like snitching – even on someone who deserves it – and Priscilla certainly deserves it!' said Hilda. 'But she'll make our lives a misery if we don't.'

'Mm,' said Katie thoughtfully. Then her brow cleared. 'I know what! We'll boycott the next meeting. Then, next day, when the sixth have been left high and dry, wondering why no one's turned up, we'll go along to the head girls and tell them all about Priscilla.'

'Good idea,' said Dora. 'Daphne and I'll shoot off to the second and third forms and put them in the picture as well. Oh, and someone had better keep an eye on *her.*' She nodded scornfully in Joan's direction and the girl cowered miserably in her chair.

'Yes,' agreed Daphne. 'Otherwise we'll have her running off to Priscilla as soon as our backs are turned to warn her of what we're planning.'

Poor Joan made no attempt to defend herself. What was the point? Seeing how unhappy the girl looked, Katie said sharply, 'Now that's enough. Go on then, twins, and remember, everyone – no matter how serious your problems are, the sixth's meeting is strictly out of bounds on Thursday.'

12

A week of shocks and surprises

The following day, Pat had a surprise when Morag approached her in the dormitory before breakfast and said in a low voice, 'Can you spare me a moment, Pat?'

'I suppose so,' she answered, not very graciously, for she was thoroughly fed up with the girl's sullen manner.

'I just wanted to apologize,' said Morag quietly. 'I was really rude to you yesterday. In fact, I've been rude and aggressive to everyone, behaving like a spoilt, stupid kid.' She gave a sad smile and went on, 'I just hope you haven't given up on me altogether, because things are going to be different from now on.'

'Well, you don't know how pleased I am to hear that!' said Pat, amazed and unable to stop herself from responding to the girl's infectious smile. She admired Morag for having the courage to own up to her faults and apologize so unreservedly. 'What's brought this on?'

'Oh, Carlotta gave me a good talking to, and suddenly I seemed to see things in a different light,' answered Morag.

And, certainly, she seemed like a different person this morning, thought Pat. Good one, Carlotta!

The rest of the sixth were astonished to see Pat and

Morag come into breakfast together, chattering away like old friends and Doris, as she said later, almost fainted into her cereal when the Scottish girl beamed round the table and greeted everyone with a cheerful 'Good morning'. Isabel blinked and, as her twin sat down beside her, said, 'She *looks* like Morag and she *sounds* like Morag, but I think she's been taken over by an alien being!'

'Idiot,' laughed Pat, helping herself to toast. 'Hey, where's Alison? Don't tell me she's still in bed.'

'Either that or she's curling her hair, or painting her toe-nails,' said Isabel.

'Oh, well, I'm not going to look for her. Alison's old enough now to be responsible for herself, and if she misses breakfast, it's her own fault.'

Alison was neither asleep nor gazing into her mirror. She had been waylaid by Joan Terry, who she had found waiting for her outside the dormitory.

'Joan!' she exclaimed, surprised and none too pleased. 'What are you doing here? You really aren't supposed to be in this area, you know.'

'Oh, Alison, don't be mad with me,' said Joan, her brown eyes pleading. 'I came to see if there was anything you might need doing in your dormitory. Perhaps I could make your bed, or tidy your locker or . . .'

'My bed is made and I'll tidy my locker at break-time,' said Alison with unusual firmness. 'You know it's the rule that we do those things ourselves. Matron would be absolutely furious if she thought I was getting you to do them for me.'

'But you're not – I offered,' persisted Joan. 'I like doing things for you, Alison.'

'Yes, and I appreciate it,' said Alison, feeling a bit hounded. 'But enough's enough, Joan. Now hurry, or we'll both be late for breakfast.' With that she walked briskly away before the younger girl could wear her down. Alison was well aware that hers was a weak character, and the first former had an unexpectedly determined side to her when she badly wanted to do something. And it seemed that what she most wanted to do was make a willing slave of herself to Alison. Alison liked the girl and, at first, had enjoyed the novelty of being looked up to. Now, however, it had worn thin and Joan was definitely becoming a nuisance. Fortunately, Alison managed to slip into the dining-room unnoticed by any mistress and Pat hissed, 'Where have you been?'

'I really don't want to talk about it,' snapped Alison, still feeling ruffled. 'Pass the marmalade, please.'

Pat did so, looking at her cousin in surprise. Normally Alison chattered non-stop about every trivial detail of her life to anyone who would listen. Nor was it like her to snap. She was certainly preoccupied about something, though – and why did she keep looking over at the first-form table like that?

Of course, Alison was looking out for Joan, half afraid that the girl might try to join her at the sixth's table. But the meal went on and still she didn't appear. Wherever could she have got to?

Alison found out at break-time when she slipped to the dormitory to tidy her locker.

'I'll come with you,' said Doris. 'Mine's an absolute tip and we don't want Matron dishing out another order mark.'

Both girls were in for a shock when they entered the dormitory. For on the floor lay a framed photograph of Alison's parents, which she kept on her locker, the glass smashed to pieces.

'Oh, no!' cried Doris, taking a look at Alison's white face. 'However could that have happened?'

Poor Alison was too upset to reply, though she knew who was responsible. But had Joan deliberately smashed the photograph in anger at Alison's coolness? Or had it been an accident? Stepping carefully over the broken glass, Alison pulled open the door of her locker. Not a thing out of place! So Joan had ignored her and tidied her locker after all, which meant that the photograph must have been broken by accident. That was some comfort, for Alison would have hated to think that Joan could have done it deliberately. All the same, she wished she had the girl in front of her now, because she'd like to shake her! Probably the silly kid had panicked and run off as soon as the accident happened. Doris, who had popped out to fetch a dustpan and brush, came back and exclaimed, 'Why, your locker was an absolute shambles before breakfast and now it's tidy! What *is* going on?'

As they swept up the glass Alison told her, and Doris

exclaimed, 'The nerve of her! Sneaking in here after you'd told her not to! I hope you're going to give her a rocket, Alison.'

'You can count on it!'

That afternoon Joan sought her out and owned up in a trembling voice. 'I'm so sorry, Alison. It was an accident, but I'll save all my money to buy you a new frame, honestly.'

Remembering that Joan had once said that she didn't get very much money from home, Alison's tender heart melted and she found herself patting the girl on her shoulder. 'Accidents will happen,' she said. 'Just be more careful next time.'

'I will, Alison,' said Joan, happy again now that she had been forgiven.

Only after the girl had gone did it occur to Alison that she hadn't told Joan off for disobeying her orders. What was worse, she might just take that 'next time' Alison had warned her about as an open invitation to go into her dormitory and tidy up whenever she felt like it. With a groan Alison sank down on to a chair and buried her face in her hands. Whatever had she done to deserve this?

If Alison was down in the dumps, Morag's new happiness showed no signs of abating, to the delight of the sixth form who had feared it might be a flash in the pan. The mistresses were pleased with her too, Miss Harry confiding to Mam'zelle that she had hardly believed her eyes when the girl had not only held open the door for her that morning, but had actually *smiled* at her.

'Ah, yes, even in her French she is trying hard,' said Mam'zelle beaming. 'She made so brave an effort to roll her Rs correctly yesterday.' Her smile became a little less warm. 'Sadly, she did not succeed, but no matter. At least she tries.'

Morag had indeed tried, much to the amusement of the class. Her Scottish brogue did not make for a smooth French accent and, in the common-room later, Doris had imitated her efforts, to the hilarity of the others. And Morag had laughed louder than anyone, tears pouring down her cheeks.

Doris is a real comedienne, she thought in surprise. And I've only just discovered it. She looked around at the others, all of them holding their sides helplessly. It makes me realize how little I know about *any* of the sixth really, apart from Carlotta. Well, it's time I started taking an interest in others, including the little ones. Tomorrow's meeting will be an excellent place to start.

Alas for such good intentions! At seven precisely, the sixth form gathered round the big table and waited . . . and waited. At seven-thirty Fizz looked at her watch and said with a sigh, 'Looks as though no one's coming, girls.'

'I can't understand it,' said Isabel with a frown. 'Surely the advice we dished out last week wasn't so bad that no one wants to give us another chance?'

'I think we did very well,' said Anne-Marie stoutly. 'If you ask me, something's up.'

'What?' asked Pat.

'Well, I don't know. But it's very strange that not one person has come.'

Morag cleared her throat. 'As we're at a loose end, would you mind if *I* say something? You've all been patient with me and I think I owe you an explanation as to why I behaved so badly.'

'Go ahead,' said Pat curiously.

So Morag told the rest of the sixth form what she had already confided in Carlotta, and they listened intently.

'Wow, your dad really messed things up!' said Janet in her direct way. 'I often think that someone ought to start a school for parents.'

'Yes, but maybe your stepmum won't be so bad once you really get to know her,' said Gladys thoughtfully. 'You said yourself that you'd set out to make life hard for her.'

'Well, I mean to try to get to know her better now,' said Morag, looking a little shamefaced. 'She and Dad are coming to take me out at half-term, so it'll be a chance to show her that I can act like a normal human being!'

'It's really good that you felt you could tell us all this,' said Bobby. 'It makes you belong more, somehow, knowing that you trust us enough to share your secret with us.'

'Of course!' said Doris suddenly. 'That's what these meetings are all about, aren't they? Alison, come on, share *your* problem and see what words of wisdom the sixth have to offer.'

Alison turned pink. 'I couldn't possibly! We're supposed to help the younger girls.'

'Well, it's a bad job if we can't help one of our own,' insisted Doris.

'What are you two talking about?' asked Hilary impatiently. 'Alison, is there something you're worried about?'

'Well, yes, actually,' said Alison hesitantly, and began to tell the girls about 'the Joan affair' as she had come to think of it. 'It's as though I can't turn round without finding her there,' she finished plaintively. 'If I wake up in the middle of the night I expect to find her standing by my bedside.'

'I see,' said Janet, her lips quivering as she looked at Alison rather oddly. 'Well, if you ask me . . .'

But Janet couldn't go on, overcome by a spasm of coughing so violent that Bobby had to slap her on the back.

'Er . . . I think that what Janet is trying to say,' began Hilary, in a strange, quavery voice, 'is . . . oh dear, oh I can't!' Then she burst out laughing and clutched at Doris, who promptly did the same. Alison looked offended. 'Well,' she said stiffly. 'I'm glad you think it's funny.'

'Of course we don't, Alison,' said Pat soothingly. 'It's just that . . . oh, tell her, Isabel. I can't speak!' And before her cousin's astonished gaze, Pat too creased up laughing.

The normally good-natured Alison looked fit to explode and, seeing it, Isabel patted her on the arm. 'The thing is, Alison, it's normally *you* who goes around worshipping people and now . . .' Isabel's voice cracked and Bobby went on, 'Now you're getting a taste of your own medicine. Alison, you of all people should know how to handle this situation – after all, you've been in Joan's position often enough.'

Dumbfounded, Alison thought back over her years at St Clare's. There had been Sadie, the glamorous American girl in the first form. Then Miss Quentin, the drama teacher in the second. And how badly both of them had let her down! In the fourth she had attached herself to Angela, then last year it had been Miss Willcox, the English teacher. Sadly, both Alison and Anne-Marie, who had also adored the teacher, had discovered that Miss Willcox wasn't all that she seemed. Yes, Alison had worshipped all of these people and now here was Joan doing the same to her – and she didn't like it one little bit! Crossly she glared round the table at the laughing girls. It wasn't funny at all! Well . . . maybe just a little. Slowly one corner of Alison's mouth lifted, then the other. Soon she was laughing with the others, and how they liked her for it. She might be vain and empty headed in some ways, but Alison could take a joke against herself.

'Oh,' gasped Doris, wiping her eyes. 'I don't remember when I last laughed so much. You're a good sort not to take offence, Alison.'

So the meeting broke up on a happy note but later, back in their studies, the girls began to wonder again why none of the younger girls had attended.

The head girls discovered why the following afternoon, when Katie and Hilda knocked at their study door.

'Hi, kids!' said Pat in surprise as the two entered. 'Isabel and I didn't send for you.'

'Hilda and I'd like a word with you both, please,' said Katie, and the twins frowned at her unusually grave expression. 'It's about a certain member of the sixth.'

'Go on,' said Isabel, catching Pat's eye. The same thought was in both their minds. Only one member of the sixth could have brought such a sober expression to the girls' faces – Priscilla!

So indeed it proved. As Katie and Hilda poured out their story, the twins' faces became more and more grim. 'Our class is planning a midnight party,' Hilda finished indignantly. 'And Priscilla is always hanging round outside our common-room, trying to find out the details. We're pretty sure she means to spoil it in some way.'

'Dummy!' hissed Katie, elbowing the unfortunate Hilda.

'Don't worry, Katie,' said Pat, an amused gleam in her eye. 'If Isabel and I knew when and where you were holding the party then, naturally, it would be our duty to stop it. But as we don't know anything about it, there's nothing we can do.'

Hilda and Katie exchanged delighted glances. The O'Sullivan twins were just the greatest!

'Mm,' said Isabel thoughtfully. 'I think the best thing to do is tell Priscilla exactly when and where it's to be held, then she can try to stop it.'

'Isabel!' exclaimed Pat in amazement. 'Have you gone completely mad?'

'Far from it,' said Isabel calmly. 'I was just thinking of Elsie Fanshawe. Remember her from our days in the second form, Pat?'

'Elsie Fanshawe,' repeated Pat, light dawning. 'What a great idea, Isabel.'

The first formers listened to this exchange in bewilderment. Who was Elsie Fanshawe and what did she have to do with their present predicament? They were soon to find out.

'Elsie Fanshawe was with us back in the second form – and she was every bit as spiteful and sneaky as Priscilla! She discovered that we'd planned a midnight party and decided to ruin it,' explained Pat.

'What did you do?' asked Hilda curiously.

'Spiked her guns,' said Isabel with a laugh. 'We led Elsie to believe that our party was going to be on a certain night – then secretly held it the night before. And did we have some fun the following night, slipping out of our dormitory and hiding until she had gone off to sneak to Miss Jenks. Of course, by the time Elsie and Miss Jenks came back, we were all tucked up in bed and pretending to be fast asleep.'

'Wow!' gasped Hilda. 'What a great idea!'

'Are you saying that we ought to try the same trick on Priscilla?' asked Katie, staring hard at the twins.

'It would be most improper for us to suggest anything of the kind,' replied Isabel, a twinkle in her eye. 'Isn't that right, Pat?'

'Extremely improper,' agreed Pat, with an answering twinkle. 'Of course, if Priscilla *were* to be caught out by the "Elsie" method, I'm quite sure that Miss Theobald would bar her from any of our future Thursday meetings.'

'I see,' said Katie grinning. 'Come on, Hilda. Time to call a form meeting, I think. Thanks for your help, twins.'

'Aren't they just great?' said Hilda in delight, once they were outside. 'More or less giving us permission to trick Priscilla, *and* telling us how to go about it.'

'I'll say,' agreed Katie, adding gravely, 'There are bad head girls and there are good head girls. And then there are the O'Sullivan twins. They're in a league of their own!'

A shock for Priscilla

Half-term came and went, the girls thrilled to see their parents again. Carlotta, whose own father was away, went out with Morag, her father and stepmother. Fizz's parents couldn't come either, but her older brother Harry arrived and got permission from Miss Theobald to take out both his sister and Claudine. The three of them had a great time, Harry's sense of humour being every bit as wicked as his sister's, and the two girls returned to school in high spirits.

Joan Terry earned herself another black mark with the first form when Priscilla, knowing that the younger girl's mother and father wouldn't be there, invited Joan to spend the day with her and her own parents. There was nothing Joan would rather do less, but she didn't know how to refuse. The scornful stares of her form as they watched her drive off with Priscilla seemed to burn into her skin. 'Going off to spill our secrets,' said Rita scornfully. 'Little traitor!'

'Never mind, Rita,' said Dora, with an angelic smile. 'Joan might turn out to be very useful to us – very useful indeed!'

Priscilla also intended to make use of Joan. As soon

as they returned to school and said goodby to Mr and Mrs Parsons, Priscilla took the girl aside and said smoothly, 'Now, Joan, there's a little favour you can do for me in return for your day out.'

Joan said nothing, but waited with a sinking heart for what was to come next. 'I want you to find out when and where the first form are holding their party and tell me,' said Priscilla.

'I can't!' refused Joan, horrified. 'The others would never speak to me again!'

'Well, it's up to you, of course,' Priscilla said with a shrug. 'But if I were to let slip – purely by accident, naturally – what I know about you, no one in the whole *school* would want to speak to you.'

Joan was trapped and she knew it. Priscilla had the upper hand.

'OK, Priscilla,' said Joan woodenly. 'Whatever you want.'

'Now you're being sensible.' Priscilla smiled her thin smile. 'As soon as you find anything out, let me know.'

Spying for Priscilla proved to be an unexpectedly easy task. Joan had fully expected to be left out of the party, well aware that she wasn't exactly popular with her class. But, to her surprise, the others discussed their plans quite openly in front of her.

'So, Wednesday night is party night,' said Susan one afternoon in the common-room. 'Where's it to be?'

'In here,' said Katie. 'At midnight precisely.'

Joan sat gazing unseeingly at the book open on

her lap for a few moments, then got up and quietly slipped out.

'Straight off to Priscilla, I'll bet,' said Katie. 'Follow her, Dora. We want to make sure that she delivers the message.'

Dora did so, silently, keeping her distance and darting into doorways when Joan glanced over her shoulder. Sure enough, the girl went straight to Priscilla's study. 'Mission accomplished,' said Dora, when she reported back. 'I can't get over the way Joan's acting. We ought to get our own back on *her*, as well as Priscilla.'

'We will,' promised Katie. 'After we've had our party – on *Tuesday* night – and dealt with Priscilla!'

The party was a great success, the first formers having sneaked out of their dormitory without waking Joan. As Daphne said later, they had the most fantastic time, wolfing down crisps, sausage rolls, cakes and biscuits, all washed down with gallons of lemonade. A few of them regretted it next morning, though, finding it impossible to get out of bed.

'I don't feel well,' complained Rita as they trooped down to breakfast.

'I'm not surprised, you pig,' said Katie. 'What do you expect after eating nearly a whole tin of biscuits?'

'Ugh, don't!' groaned Rita, screwing up her face. 'I'll be sick!'

'You will not!' said Katie firmly. 'We don't want anyone getting suspicious.' She nodded towards Joan, walking a little way in front. 'Just have a cup of tea for breakfast and don't eat anything. If Miss Roberts asks why, tell her you're trying to get rid of some of that fat!' And with a wicked grin, Katie ran off towards the dining-room, Rita, forgetting her sickness for a moment, in hot pursuit. 'I'll get you for that! Oof, sorry, Mam'zelle!'

The first formers weren't the only ones waiting in anticipation for Priscilla's downfall. Pat and Isabel had told the sixth about her behaviour towards the younger girls and they had been furious.

'She's unbelievable! We'll have to bar her from our meetings, that's for sure.'

'I just hope the first form manage to set her up and she falls for it!'

'She will,' said Isabel confidently. 'Priscilla might be sly and cunning, but she's got the brains of a flea!'

Priscilla found it easy to keep awake that night, her spiteful nature rejoicing in what was to come. At a quarter to midnight she slipped silently out of bed, put on her slippers and dressing-gown, and made her way stealthily to the first-form dormitories. Hiding in a bath-room opposite, she opened the door a crack and peeped out. The first form, who had been waiting quietly and patiently, heard the soft clicking of the door.

'OK,' whispered Katie. 'You know what to do, every-one – let's go!'

The girls put into action their carefully thought out plan. Daphne and Lucy went first, leaving the dormitory with much giggling and whispering. Winking, Daphne stopped directly outside the bathroom where Priscilla was hidden and, not troubling to lower her voice, said, 'Let's go and fetch the food! This is going to be just great!'

Priscilla waited until the girls had moved away and rounded the corner before tiptoeing after them. Sadly for her, the girl didn't realize that she, too, was being shadowed – by Dora! The strange little crocodile made its way to a cupboard near the first-form common-room, from which, with a lot of unnecessary noise, Lucy and Daphne produced a large cardboard box. It was empty, of course, but Priscilla assumed that it contained food for the party. Just then the school cat, who had been peacefully sleeping in a corner, stretched and came to life, deciding that he rather liked the look of Priscilla. Silently he padded forward, tripping her up. The girl gave a gasp and stumbled, managing to regain her balance, but losing a slipper. There was no time to retrieve it, as the first formers were coming back and she had to dart behind a long curtain.

'Time to wake the others,' said Lucy, in a carrying voice. 'Not long now to party-time!'

They walked on, voices fading and, with a sigh of relief, Priscilla left her hiding place. Now to go back for her slipper. But, to the girl's annoyance, it seemed to have vanished off the face of the earth. Well, no time to worry about that now. By the time she reached the mistresses' sleeping quarters, the girls should be in their common-room and the party well under way. But not for long, thought Priscilla, grinning to herself. She had carefully planned which mistress she would go to. Miss

Roberts! She was in charge of the first form and would, no doubt, be grateful to Priscilla for the information. Miss Roberts had a sarcastic streak, too, and would soon reduce the first formers to the status of four year olds, thought Priscilla gleefully.

Stepping out of the dark shadows, Dora smiled to herself as she tapped Priscilla's slipper against the palm of her hand. She had a fair idea of the girl's plans which, unfortunately for Priscilla, didn't coincide with her own at all.

Ah, there was Miss Roberts' room, next door to Mam'zelle's. Priscilla moved towards it and raised her hand to knock. But, before it descended, something flew past her shoulder and hit Mam'zelle's door with a resounding thud. Everything seemed to happen at once after that. She heard the sound of running footsteps along the corridor, Mam'zelle's sharp *'Tiens*!' from behind her door and another voice crying, 'What on earth was that?'

Stooping to pick up the missile that had caused all the commotion, Priscilla was amazed to discover that it was her lost slipper. Suddenly Mam'zelle's door opened and, at the sight of Priscilla standing there with the incriminating slipper in her hand, the French teacher cried, '*Mon dieu*, what is the meaning of this? How dare you come here at night to throw footwear at my door? Miss Harry, come! See who is responsible for this outrage!'

The girl's jaw dropped in dismay as her own form

mistress appeared behind Mam'zelle. She hadn't known that Miss Harry was using the spare bed in Mam'zelle's room while her own room was being redecorated. Wicked little Dora had known it, though, and planned accordingly. The hot-tempered Mam'zelle and Miss Harry, who knew Priscilla's underhand ways only too well, would see to it that she got what she deserved.

'I trust you have some explanation for this extraordinary behaviour?' Miss Harry demanded, so coldly that Priscilla shook. There was nothing for it but to explain about the party, though she would far rather have told Miss Roberts. As she told her tale, the expressions on the faces of the two mistresses grew more contemptuous.

'Ha! You come to sneak!' said Mam'zelle scornfully. 'You have no honour, no decency.'

'None at all,' agreed Miss Harry, looking at the red-faced girl with dislike. 'Well, I suppose we'd better investigate, Mam'zelle. And for your sake, Priscilla, I just hope you've got your facts right.'

It was a very deflated Priscilla who followed the two mistresses to the first-form common-room, cowering back in the shadows as Miss Harry threw open the door and snapped on the light.

'I – I don't understand,' spluttered the girl, staring in horror at the empty room. 'They must have decided to hold it in the dormitory instead.'

But when they reached the dormitory it was in darkness, with only the sounds of deep breathing and an occasional gentle snore to be heard.

'Who's there?' asked Katie sleepily. 'Miss Roberts, is it you?'

'No, *ma petite*, it is I, Mam'zelle,' said the French mistress. 'And the good Miss Harry.'

'Is something wrong?' asked Katie.

'Very wrong,' said Miss Harry, with an angry look at Priscilla. 'But it's nothing for you to worry about, Katie. Go back to sleep now, dear.'

In fact, very few of the first formers had been asleep, all of them eager to learn the outcome of their trick. They were rewarded as they heard Miss Harry say to the crestfallen Priscilla, 'Thanks to your spite, Mam'zelle and I have had a disturbed night for nothing. Now, as you've done a little sneaking tonight – quite wrongly as it turns out – I'll be doing some of my own tomorrow. On you! Report to the head after breakfast!'

A bad time for the sixth

Priscilla was in trouble – big trouble! The whisper flew round the school the next morning and no one felt the slightest bit sorry for her. The girl herself was furious, guessing that she had been tricked – and that stupid little Joan had been in on it, feeding her false information. Well, she'd be sorry.

Joan was already sorry. She knew what Priscilla must be thinking and she had been taunted by the first formers that morning.

'Thanks for helping us set Priscilla up, Joan,' Susan had said cheerfully.

'Yes, we'll know who to turn to next time we're looking for a mug,' sneered Daphne.

'Dummy!' laughed Dora scornfully. 'Did you really think we'd let you in on our secret? You're not one of us!'

'Go somewhere else if you want to cry!' said Katie impatiently, as Joan began to sniff. 'Maybe your good friend Priscilla will comfort you.'

Priscilla was feeling sorely in need of comfort herself, after a long and painful interview with Miss Theobald. Every defect in the girl's character – and the head had found many – was discussed at length.

'You learnt that the first form were to hold a party and decided to spoil it,' said the head icily. 'But instead of going to the girls yourself and nipping it in the bud, you wanted to wait until the party had started, then inform on them. I'm glad that they outsmarted you! You're a troublemaker, Priscilla, and this time you've made trouble for yourself. I only hope that this will make you look at yourself long and hard, and that you'll make some attempt to change your ways. I've no choice but to recommend to the head girls that you be banned from their weekly meetings, since you're clearly not fit to deal with anyone's problems until you've sorted your own out. Go now, Priscilla, and if you're brought before me again this term, the consequences will be severe!'

Another girl might have taken Miss Theobald's words to heart, taken the opportunity to try to overcome the flaws in her character. Priscilla was too weak to do this, instead feeling bitter and resentful. And her bitterness was directed towards those who were the cause of her disgrace, as she saw it. Her first act, on leaving the head's office, was to find Joan.

The girl was standing alone in the courtyard, a forlorn figure as she watched the other first formers laughing together. If only there was someone she could confide in. Someone kind and understanding – like Alison. But the thought of her idol turning from her in disgust when she heard Joan's awful secret was worse than anything, so the girl kept it to herself, growing more withdrawn and unhappy.

'Joan, there you are! Come here!'

She turned to see Priscilla standing at the corner and went over.

'Well, you and your classmates made a complete fool of me, didn't you?' said Priscilla angrily. 'You'll pay for it, though! I warned you what would happen if you crossed me.'

'But I wasn't in on it!' protested Joan, scared. 'The others guessed that you'd try and find out about the party from me and used me.'

Looking down into the first former's scared face, Priscilla believed her. 'All right then, tell me whose idea it was,' demanded the older girl, taking Joan by the shoulders. 'Those cheeky Lacey twins, I suppose – or Katie, maybe?'

'Ow, you're hurting me,' squealed Joan, struggling to escape from Priscilla's long, bony fingers. 'All right, I'll tell! I overheard Katie saying this morning that it was the sixth's idea. They put Katie up to it.'

'The sixth!' Priscilla's hands fell from Joan's shoulders, her face darkening with fury. She was so angry that she shook. How could they! To side with the first form against her and plan her downfall! Well, if they thought they were going to get away with it, they could think again. She'd get her own back on the lot of them!

Shortly afterwards, strange things began to happen in the sixth form. It started with Pat and Isabel, who had just bought their mother a bottle of her favourite perfume for her birthday. But when the time came for them to wrap it up and post it, it had completely vanished.

'I'm sure I put it in this cupboard,' said Isabel, scratching her head.

'You did,' Pat said. 'I saw you. But it's certainly not there now.'

The perfume didn't turn up, and the twins had to spend what money they had left on a box of chocolates for their mother instead, which didn't please them at all.

The following day, Hilary's watch disappeared, along with Janet's fountain pen. Within a few days nearly all of the sixth had lost something.

'Lost!' snorted Bobby as she discussed the matter with the twins, Janet and Hilary in the common-room one afternoon. 'We all know that our things haven't just been mislaid. Let's face it, girls, they've been stolen!'

'I think you're right,' admitted Pat reluctantly. Try as they might, she and Isabel had been unable to come up with another explanation. 'But who could it be?'

'There is one rather obvious suspect,' said Janet drily.

'Priscilla!' chorused the others.

'She's got the motive,' said Isabel. 'She was absolutely furious about being barred from our meetings.'

'And she'll be out to get her own back, if I know anything about her,' said Hilary.

'Hold on a minute!' put in Bobby, who had been looking thoughtful. 'It can't be Priscilla. Anne-Marie had a fiver taken from her study last night, while she was at that debate with the fifth, and Priscilla was there too.'

'Are you sure?' asked Pat.

'Absolutely. I was there myself, and Priscilla was sitting right in front of Anne-Marie and me. I remember particularly, because I had to tell her to move her big head,' Bobby said.

'Couldn't she have slipped out early or something?' asked Janet.

Bobby shook her head. 'She was already in her seat when Anne-Marie arrived, and didn't move until we'd left. Sorry, folks, but it looks as though that rules Priscilla out.'

'Then who?' asked Janet uncomfortably. 'I'd hate to think it could be one of the others who've come up through the school with us.'

'Of course it isn't,' Hilary said firmly.

'Well, that only leaves Morag and Fizz,' said Isabel. 'And I can't believe either of them would do such a thing.'

'Just a second!' Bobby snapped her fingers suddenly, looking excited. 'There is one member of our class who hasn't had anything taken yet – Alison!'

'Hang on, Bobby!' said Pat, firing up. 'I know Alison's got her faults, but she doesn't have a dishonest bone in her body. She'd never . . .'

'I'm not accusing Alison, you feather-brain!' interrupted Bobby, thumping Pat on the arm. 'I know she's straight.'

'Oh. Sorry, Bobby,' said Pat, looking a little sheepish. 'What *are* you suggesting, then?'

137

'That the thief is someone who has a soft spot for Alison and wants to leave her out of this campaign that she's waging against the rest of us.'

'Joan!' cried Isabel, adding, as the others stared at her, 'Well, she's always in and out of Alison's study, so it would be easy for her to nip into ours when they're empty, and take something.'

'That's true,' Pat said. 'But what on earth could that little shrimp have against us?'

'Search me,' sighed Hilary. 'I've a feeling we're on the right track, though. Look, let's get Alison in and see what she thinks. She knows Joan better than any of us.'

Janet sped off to fetch Alison from her study, and within moments the two girls were back. Swiftly Pat told her cousin what they had been discussing, and the girl's blue eyes widened.

'No!' she protested, shocked. 'She's a strange girl in some ways, but I'd never have thought her a thief.'

'Well, she's the only person we can think of,' said Janet. 'So one of us ought to tackle her about it.'

'I think it ought to be you, Alison,' said Isabel at once.

'Oh, no!' Alison shook her head firmly. 'You, or Pat, or Hilary are much better at that kind of thing than I am.'

'But Joan doesn't look up to us in the way she looks up to you,' Pat pointed out. 'Come on, Alison! Do it for the sixth.'

'Oh, all right. But there's something I need to do first. Miss Roberts has taken the first form on a nature-walk this afternoon, hasn't she?'

'That's right,' said Pat. 'You'll have to wait until after tea to see Joan.'

'Good,' Alison said. 'Because first I intend to search her locker.'

'Alison!' cried Hilary. 'You can't go snooping around in the first-form dormitories.'

'Oh, yes I can! If I'm to accuse her of stealing – which, by the way, I am still not convinced of – then I'd feel far happier if I had some proof.'

'Well, if you put it like that, I suppose it might not be such a bad idea,' agreed Bobby. 'I'll come with you, Alison, and keep look-out.'

'Now, which do you suppose is Joan's bed?' mused Alison, once she and Bobby were in the dormitory. Then she spotted a pair of shoes beside one of the beds. 'Those are hers, I'm sure of it!'

'Well, get on with it!' said Bobby impatiently from the doorway. 'If Matron catches us poking around in here, we're in deep trouble.'

So Alison opened the locker beside the bed and removed a wash-bag, two books – aha, what was that, right at the back? Her fingers touched a box and she pulled it forward, removing the lid. 'Bobby!' she gasped. 'Take a look at this!'

With a swift glance up and down the corridor, Bobby left her post, giving a low whistle as she saw the contents of the box. 'The twins' perfume,' she said. 'Hilary's watch – and the record I bought last week! The little thief!'

'I can't believe it,' said Alison sadly.

'Never mind,' said Bobby kindly, resting a hand on her shoulder. 'At least you won't have to tackle her about it now. With this lot as proof, we can go straight to the head.'

'If you don't mind, Bobby, I'd rather talk to her first,' said Alison soberly. 'I just want to know *why*!'

Bobby shrugged. 'Fair enough. Now we'd better put everything back just as we found it. We don't want Joan to guess we're on to her until we're good and ready.'

Alison was on tenterhooks until after tea, very little of which she managed to eat. Then she sent someone to find Joan. Alison studied the girl closely when she arrived, noticing that, despite an afternoon in the fresh air, her cheeks were pale and there were dark circles beneath her eyes. She managed to smile, though, and said brightly, 'Hi, Alison! Did you want me?'

'Sit down, Joan,' said Alison seriously. 'I want to talk to you.' Then, in her mind, she ran over the little speech she had rehearsed. It was no use beating about the bush, she had decided. She must come straight to the point. 'Joan, we know that you've been stealing things from the sixth formers,' she said directly. 'I want to know why.'

If Joan had looked pale before, she was positively white now. For a moment she was tempted to deny the accusation, then she saw the grave look in Alison's eyes and knew that it was no use. 'How did you find out?' she asked bleakly.

'We suspected you because nothing was taken from me,' answered Alison. 'Then I searched your locker this afternoon and found the things that the others had missed. Oh, Joan, why did you do it?'

The first former buried her face in her hands. 'I'm sorry, Alison!' she cried. 'So sorry. I've never done anything like it before.'

'Then why now? Come on, Joan, you must tell me everything if I'm to help you.' Alison's tone was kind and Joan looked up.

'Oh, if only you could. But I'm in such a mess and I just can't see a way out.'

Alison said nothing, but took the girl's hand and squeezed it gently.

'Someone else made me take those things,' said Joan at last. 'Someone who's got it in for the sixth. I can't tell you who.'

'You don't need to,' Alison said grimly. 'There's only one person I can think of who's got something against us – Priscilla Parsons!'

'Oh!' Joan became very agitated and began to cry. 'Now I've made things worse!'

'Well, I don't see how things *can* get worse,' said Alison frankly. 'Joan, what made you agree to do such a thing? You must have known it was wrong. Why didn't you tell someone what was happening?'

'I couldn't,' sobbed the first former. 'I have to do

what Priscilla wants. You see, she knows something about me – something bad – and threatened to tell the whole school.'

Alison's gentle blue eyes grew hard and angry. Just wait until the others heard this. Then Priscilla would be sorry.

'Joan, whatever Priscilla knows, you *must* tell me,' she said urgently. 'Once your secret's out, her hold over you will be broken.'

'I know, but you'll hate me, and I couldn't stand that,' hiccuped Joan, dabbing at her eyes.

'Of course I won't hate you!' cried Alison. 'Please, Joan! This is the only way we can stop Priscilla.'

Joan took a deep breath and said bravely, 'It's my dad. He's been accused of embezzling money from the firm he worked for, and now he's in prison awaiting trial. Alison, he didn't do it, I know he didn't! But everyone at home knows all about it, including Priscilla. Some people have been kind and stood by us, but others haven't and it's all been so horrid for Mum and me.'

'Oh, Joan,' whispered Alison, absolutely horrified. 'What a burden to carry all by yourself. And on top of that, to have Priscilla taking advantage of your misery. Well, that's one thing I *can* put a stop to!'

Alison got purposefully to her feet and Joan said, in alarm, 'Where are you going? What's going to happen?'

The older girl patted Joan's arm reassuringly. 'I need to discuss this with the others,' she said. 'But you can trust them not to spread it around. And nothing terrible is going to happen to you, I promise. Now, Joan, I want you to go back to the first form and, if you should bump into Priscilla, say nothing about all this. That girl isn't going to know what hit her!'

Things are sorted out

Alison shot off to the studies and rounded up the sixth formers – all except Priscilla, of course. In the common-room she told them Joan's story and, as she had expected, they were outraged.

'I'd like to get my hands on her!' cried Doris, shaking with anger. 'I hate bullying more than anything!'

'She's evil!' shuddered Anne-Marie. 'To use one of the kids like that.'

'Where is she?' demanded Bobby. 'Fetch her, some-one, and we'll show her what happens to people who pick on little kids!'

'OK, calm down, everyone!' Pat raised her voice. 'I understand how you're all feeling, because I feel just the same. But we have to do this by the book. I think Isabel and I ought to see Miss Theobald first. Alison, you'd better come with us. Well done for getting to the bottom of this.'

'Yes, nice work!' called out some of the others, and Alison flushed. Used to being the class feather-head for years, it was rather nice to be praised for once. Fortunately the head was in and she listened gravely as the three girls explained the extraordinary happenings in the sixth form and the parts Priscilla and Joan had played.

'What will happen to Joan?' asked Alison anxiously, once they had finished.

'Nothing very terrible, though I'll have a serious talk with her, of course. I think she's been punished quite enough already, poor child,' said Miss Theobald heavily. 'There's only one person to blame in all this, and I intend to deal with her severely. Thank you, twins – and Alison. I'm very pleased with the way you've all handled this matter. Now, send Priscilla to see me, please.'

Priscilla was puzzled when told that the head wanted to see her, but not concerned. What was there to worry about, after all? She had got her own back on the sixth, and no one was any the wiser. Perhaps Miss Theobald had changed her mind and was going to allow her to attend the meetings again. But one look at the head's stern face was enough to tell the girl that she was in very serious trouble. Miss Theobald wasted no time in telling her why she had been sent for, watching without pity as the girl turned white and she began to shake.

'You're a disgrace to St Clare's, Priscilla. What upsets me most about the whole affair is that you used blackmail on a younger girl to carry out your nasty little schemes.'

Priscilla flinched and the head went on ominously, 'Yes, blackmail is an ugly word, isn't it? And an ugly act – a criminal act!'

The girl was terrified now, and asked in a shaky voice, 'What will happen to me?'

'Hopefully you'll learn from this experience and use that knowledge to become a better person in the future,' said Miss Theobald. 'But I cannot keep you at St Clare's, Priscilla. I've already called your parents and they are on their way.'

Priscilla stared at the head, too shocked to speak. Expelled! The disgrace of it! What would her mum and dad say? Then she began to cry, pleading, 'Miss Theobald, give me another chance, please. I'll make it up to the sixth form, and to Joan.'

But Miss Theobald shook her head. 'It's too late, Priscilla. I have the welfare of the younger girls to consider. This is for your sake, too, because I'm afraid that what you've done is something the others will never be able to forgive or forget. Now go and pack, and try to accept your punishment bravely. It could be the making of you.'

At last the door closed behind the girl and Miss Theobald heaved a sigh. Thank goodness that, for every girl like Priscilla, there were dozens like the O'Sullivan twins.

Joan was sent for too, but the head spoke to her gently and reassuringly. 'It's never any good bottling things up, Joan – as I think you've learnt to your cost. In future, if something is troubling you, do talk to someone about it.'

'I will, Miss Theobald,' promised the girl earnestly, and left the head's room feeling as though a huge weight had been lifted from her shoulders. If only she could put things right for her father. And if only she could settle things with the rest of her form. Well, there was nothing she could do for her father, sadly, but maybe there was a solution to the second of her problems. Miss Theobald was right – she would go to the sixth's next meeting and see what they could do for her.

The sixth form was a much happier place without Priscilla in it. Only Angela and Mirabel, who were taking their exams that week, were down in the dumps. They grew very short tempered with the strain of it, but the others understood how they were feeling and made allowances for them.

'All the same, I'll be glad when it's over,' said Hilary, who had broken in on Mirabel's studies to ask if she felt like a walk into town and got her head bitten off for her trouble. 'Let's just hope they pass after all this.'

Miss Harry gave out the results in class the following week, a solemn look on her face that made both girls' hearts sink as she handed them identical brown envelopes. Silently, the two girls opened them. Then Mirabel gave a yell. 'I've passed! And I've got the grades I wanted. I've passed! How about you, Angela?'

'Yes!' A wide grin spread over Angela's lovely face. 'Yes! I can't believe it! And you too! Well done, Mirabel!'

'Well done yourself!' returned Mirabel gruffly, turning pink. Then Angela surprised the class, and herself, by giving Mirabel a sudden hug, and the whole form erupted, gathering round to congratulate the girls and thumping them on the back, while Miss Harry watched, smiling.

'I'd just like to apologize to everyone for being a bit short this last week,' said Mirabel frankly. 'Exam nerves. I'll make it up to all of you.'

'The same goes for me, too,' agreed Angela, behaving pleasantly for once. She was thrilled that she could go to finishing school, of course, but she also felt an unexpected sense of achievement at having worked so hard and succeeded at something. Even spoilt Angela was feeling the effects of St Clare's.

There was good news for Carlotta that day, too. True to her word, Miss Theobald had written to the girl's father, urging him most strongly to reconsider his decision about sending Carlotta to finishing school. Mr Brown had been impressed by both her words, and her high regard for his daughter, and decided that if Miss Theobald thought Carlotta was fine as she was, that was good enough for him. Both the head and Carlotta were delighted to receive letters from him informing them of his change of heart, and the sixth form were almost as thrilled by Carlotta's news as they were over Angela and Mirabel's success.

'Things are really going our way,' commented Pat happily at the beginning of their next Thursday meeting. 'Priscilla's gone, and as for Morag – well, she's like a different person.'

'Yes, we've solved our own problems,' said Hilary. 'Now let's see what we can do for the kids. Wonder who'll be first tonight?'

It was Joan, looking a little apprehensive. The sixth

formers had all felt extremely sorry for her when Alison told them about her father, and none of them blamed her in the least for her part in the thefts. Isabel smiled and said pleasantly, 'What can we do for you, Joan?'

'I'm not very popular with the girls in my form,' said Joan, getting straight to the point. 'None of them likes me because I always seemed to side with Priscilla, and she made me tell her about the midnight party. Daphne and Dora have really got it in for me, and I just can't seem to change their opinion.'

'Well, I reckon if anyone deserves a chance, it's you, Joan,' said Carlotta. 'The first form aren't a bad lot, and I'm sure if you explained about your dad they'd understand.'

'I couldn't,' said Joan, with a firm shake of the head. 'I don't mind you knowing, because I know you'll keep it to yourselves, but I couldn't stand it if the whole school knew. It's bad enough at home, with all the stares and whispers, but I thought that here I'd be able to get away from it.'

'Hmm, we need to talk this through, I think,' said Pat. 'Joan, go back to the common-room and we'll send for you soon. In the meantime, try not to worry.'

'Wow, this is a tricky one,' said Janet. 'You can't really blame the first form for thinking the worst of Joan.'

'Actually, I've an idea,' said Isabel, going to the door. Putting her head out, she called to a passing second former. 'Sheila! Fetch Daphne and Dora Lacey for me, would you?'

'Will do, Isabel,' answered the girl, and sped off.

'What are you up to?' asked Pat suspiciously, but Isabel shook her head. 'Just wait and see, Pat,' she said.

'Well, if it isn't the Heavenly Twins,' said Bobby, grinning at the identical, innocent faces when Daphne and Dora appeared.

'Are we in trouble?' they asked in unison.

'Not so far as we know,' answered Isabel drily. 'But we need you to do us a favour. You see, girls, there's a girl in your class who's not very happy, and we want you to look after her, try to cheer her up a bit.'

The twins glanced at one another in surprise. They hadn't had the slightest inkling as to why the sixth had sent for them, but they certainly hadn't expected this! It was quite an honour really, being singled out and entrusted with such an important task, thought Dora. Evidently Daphne thought so too. Her head high and a note of pride in her voice she answered, 'Leave it to us, Isabel. Who is it?'

'Joan Terry,' answered Isabel, watching the two girls' expressions carefully.

'Oh, no!' wailed Dora. 'Anyone but her. She's so wet, and the most awful snitch besides. Honestly, Isabel, you don't know the half of it.'

'I'm afraid it's you two who don't know the half of it,' put in Pat. 'Now listen! Joan has serious problems at home. I can't tell you what, exactly, because that would be breaking a confidence. Just take my word for it that she's going through a very bad time at the moment. To make things worse, Priscilla knew all about Joan's troubles and threatened to spread gossip about her round the school if she didn't do everything Priscilla said.'

The two pairs of round blue eyes grew rounder still. 'We had no idea,' said Daphne in dismay.

'If only we'd known, we wouldn't have been quite so hard on her,' added Dora, looking a little ashamed of herself.

'Well, now's your chance to make up for it,' said Pat.

'We will,' said Dora fervently.

'Yes, you can count on us. We'll cheer her up, all right,' Daphne promised.

'I'll just bet you will,' said Bobby with a grin. 'Now shove off – and behave yourselves!'

16

A lovely end to the term

The Lacey twins were as good as their word, changing completely towards Joan and including her in everything. She was a little wary of their friendship at first, suspecting them of some trick, but once she realized they were in earnest, she opened up a little. They, in turn, were happily surprised to discover that Joan had a wicked sense of humour. And if she was a little quiet and withdrawn at times, the twins remembered the problems Isabel had spoken of and did their best to take her out of herself. The rest of the first form followed the twins' lead and Joan's popularity increased by the day as the business with Priscilla was forgotten. Alison, too, was pleased, for although Joan still came faithfully to do her jobs, the girl no longer hung round her so much.

One day towards the end of term, Joan was summoned to Miss Theobald's room. Rather fearfully she went in, hoping that the head hadn't got to hear about the trick she and the twins were planning for Mam'zelle's next French lesson. It seemed not, for Miss Theobald was wearing her most charming smile. 'Sit down, dear,' she said warmly. 'I have wonderful news. Your mother has called me to say that your father's name has been cleared. Evidently another man has confessed to taking the money he was accused of stealing.'

'Oh, Miss Theobald, is this really true?' breathed Joan, hardly daring to believe it.

'Indeed it is,' laughed the head. 'So you can look forward to the holidays, knowing that your family will be complete again. Now, your mother wants you to ring her, and she'll give you all the details. I'll go outside and give you some privacy.'

After a laughter-and-tear-filled conversation with her mother, Joan practically sprinted back to class, bumping into a group of sixth formers on the way.

'Hey, slow down, Joan!' called out Janet. 'Are you training for the Olympics, or something?'

'Sorry! Oh, Janet, Bobby, twins – I've just had the most incredible news!' said the happy first former, her face glowing. 'My dad's name has been cleared. Another man's confessed to taking the money. I *knew* he was innocent!'

'That's just wonderful!' exclaimed Isabel. 'I'm really pleased for you, Joan.'

'That goes for all of us,' agreed Bobby, with her ready smile. 'Good for you!' Joan went happily on her way and Pat said, 'Suddenly there seems an awful lot to celebrate, what with Angela and Mirabel's exams and Carlotta not having to go to that awful finishing school.'

'I was thinking that we ought to do something to mark Hilary's leaving, too,' said Bobby. 'You know she won't be coming back next term.'

There was a subdued silence as everyone digested

this. Hilary was a very popular girl, and St Clare's just wouldn't be the same without her.

'Let's have a party!' cried Pat. 'A celebration and a leaving party for Hilary all in one.'

'Great idea!' said Isabel at once. 'What a shame we're too old and responsible to have a midnight party. That really would finish the term off with a bang.'

'Wouldn't it just,' sighed Janet. Then she brightened. 'I bet if we asked Miss Theobald, she'd let us hold a party in the common-room one evening. We could get in some food and it would be just like a midnight-do, but earlier.'

'Yes!' chorused the others. 'That would be fantastic!'

'Let's not say anything to Hilary,' suggested Bobby. 'We'll make it a surprise party.'

'Better and better,' said Isabel happily. 'Come on, let's find the others – all except Hilary, of course – and make plans. We haven't got long.'

Miss Theobald was delighted to give permission for the party, and the evening before the end of term saw the sixth busily setting out plates of food in the common-room. What a surprise Hilary would have had if she had been able to see what was going on in there! Claudine and Fizz had decorated the room with colourful paper streamers, and a checked cloth covered the big table on which stood plates loaded with sandwiches, sausage rolls, crisps – and everything the girls liked best!

'I'm starving,' said Doris, looking longingly at the

food. 'Do you think I could have just *one* sandwich?'

'Certainly not,' said Pat sternly, slapping her hand away. 'We've all missed out on tea today.'

The girls had all voted not to eat at tea-time, in anticipation of the evening's party. Only Hilary was in the dark – which was where Carlotta and Morag had come in. The two of them had taken Hilary out riding late that afternoon, pretending to get hopelessly lost on the way back to the stables and arriving back at school far too late for tea.

Just my luck! Hilary had thought crossly. I'm starving, too, after that ride. I wonder if Doris has any of those biscuits left?

But Doris was nowhere to be found – and nor were any of the other sixth formers. What was more, when Hilary tried the door to the common-room, it was locked. It really was very strange! By eight o'clock, Hilary was feeling lonely and fed-up – not to mention hungry – when Claudine suddenly burst into her study.

'Ah, Hilary, you must come to the common-room at once!' she demanded.

'The common-room's locked,' said Hilary, puzzled. 'I tried the door earlier.'

'Now it is open. Please, Hilary,' Claudine pulled the girl to her feet. 'Something most strange is happening in there.'

'Heavens, what?' asked Hilary, following the girl.

But Claudine took refuge in a torrent of rapid, excited French, which she kept up until they reached the common-room. Then she threw open the door. All was dark and silent as Hilary stepped inside, then Claudine switched on the light.

'Surprise!'

Hilary gasped, hardly able to believe her eyes. 'How fantastic! Oh, what angels you all are!' she cried. 'You must have worked like slaves! It looks gorgeous!'

'Well, we couldn't let you go without a proper send-off,' said Bobby. 'Pat, Isabel – I think you have something for Hilary before we eat.'

The head girls came forward, carrying between them a large, flat parcel, which they handed to the surprised girl.

'A little memento of the happy times we've all shared,' said Pat, smiling.

'Yes, we can't have you forgetting all about us,' added Isabel.

'As if!' Hilary exclaimed, tearing open the parcel. 'Oh, this is just lovely!'

Miss Theobald had arranged for the sixth formers and the teachers to have a group photograph taken, then everyone had clubbed together to buy a silver frame for it. The mistresses had even contributed towards the food, and many of them had promised to look in during the evening. Hilary was a very popular girl. Tears misted her eyes now as she looked at the photograph and said in a choked voice, 'I'm going to miss you all so much.'

Alison, always easily moved, gave a loud sniff and

Doris called out, 'Don't start blubbing, Hilary! You'll set us all off!'

'Yes, this is supposed to be a happy occasion,' Anne-Marie put in. 'Come on, everyone – let's party!'

And party they did! The piles of food disappeared rapidly as the hungry girls attacked it. Then the table was pushed back against the wall, a record player was produced and the girls held an impromptu dance. Mam'zelle arrived just as the dancing began and joined in enthusiastically, keeping the girls in stitches.

'Go, Mam'zelle!' yelled Bobby. 'Isn't she just great?'

'I'll say,' agreed Carlotta. 'What a brilliant end to the term this is, Bobby!'

There was one more surprise to come before the evening was over. Worn out with dancing, the girls had turned the music down low and were sitting about chatting as they sipped ginger beer and lemonade from paper cups.

'This certainly beats day school,' declared Fizz. 'Nothing like this ever happened there.'

A sudden silence descended and all the girls stared at her. The voice in which she had spoken was quite different from the Cockney accent they had become used to.

'Heavens, Fizz, have you been taking elocution lessons or something?' asked Mirabel.

Fizz laughed, turning slightly red, and shook her head. 'No. I'm afraid I haven't been quite honest with you. I hope you won't be mad with me, but it was all in a good cause.'

'Whatever do you mean?' asked Pat, quite unable to get used to the girl's new, refined tone.

'What I told you about not fitting in at my day school was quite true. But it wasn't because my family had suddenly become wealthy,' Fizz explained. 'You see, we've *always* been wealthy. My parents are the Duke and Duchess of Delchester and I'm *Lady* Phyllis Bentley.'

The girls listened with their mouths agape. Many of them felt rather disappointed in Fizz for having lied to them, and the girl saw it in their faces.

'Please don't judge me too harshly!' she pleaded. 'Not until you've heard me out.'

'Go on,' said Janet coolly.

'Well, until last year, I was educated at home by a tutor. Then my parents decided I ought to mix with people my age more, and sent me to our local school.'

She grimaced and Alison asked, 'Weren't you popular there?'

'Oh, I was popular, all right,' said Fizz drily. 'But for all the wrong reasons. Everyone wanted to be friends with Lady Phyllis, to be invited to her big house, and meet the Duke and Duchess! But no one really wanted to take the trouble to get to know *me*, Fizz, as a person.'

'Wow!' exclaimed Bobby. 'Well, it just goes to show that the upper classes have their problems too.'

'Yes, having everyone want to know you because of *what* you are rather than *who* you are isn't much fun,' said Fizz with a sigh. 'So I decided I wanted to start afresh, somewhere no one knew about my parents or my title, to see if anyone really did like me for myself.'

'And we do, Lady Fizz,' Claudine spoke up. 'Very much.'

'Does Miss Theobald know about this?' asked Isabel.

'Yes, and she agreed to it.' Fizz grinned. 'You've all been so sweet to me that now I can come clean – and I'm glad of it, too, because I haven't felt good about not being straight with you. Well, what's the verdict? Am I forgiven?'

There was a moment's silence – then a roar of agreement, all of the girls seeing Fizz's point; they were delighted that she wanted to be accepted as one of them. All but one girl, and that was Angela. She turned crimson with mortification when she remembered how she had snubbed Fizz and looked down on her. And all the time her family were aristocrats! How impressed her mother would have been if she could have gone home tomorrow and boasted that Lady Phyllis Bentley was her friend. Instead, she was probably the most unpopular girl in the class, as far as Fizz was concerned. She watched the girl now, joking with Claudine and laughing as Janet teased, 'Come on, Lady Fizz, we have to clear up before bed-time – we've given the help the night off!'

Despite their late night, the girls were up bright and early the next morning, looking forward to the holidays.

'Our first term as head girls over already,' said Pat rather sadly, as she and Isabel packed. 'Hasn't it just flown?'

'Yes, but the holidays will go even faster,' replied

Isabel. 'And then we'll be back. Hey, Claudine, those are *my* slippers you're packing! Were you thinking of taking them on holiday to France?'

'*Pardon*, Isabel,' apologized the French girl, handing them back. 'My head is in the sky today.'

'The clouds, dope, not the sky!' laughed Pat. 'Why's that, Claudine?'

'Because I do not go to France this holiday,' said Claudine. 'I have been invited to stay with Fizz and her so-wonderful parents. And I am to go to the ball they are holding. Ah, I shall probably be engaged to a lord, at the very least, when I return next term.'

The others laughed loudly – apart from Angela, who could hardly contain herself as she heard this. If only she hadn't been such a snob, she might be going home with Fizz for the holidays, a guest at the Duke and Duchess's ball, instead of that awful Claudine.

Hilary, meanwhile, who had finished her packing earlier, was looking out of the window with rather a wistful expression.

'Everything all right?' asked Pat gently, going across to her.

'Yes, I was just thinking back over the last six years,' said the girl. 'In some ways I wish I was a first former again, with it all to look forward to.'

'Yes, but you've a whole new life ahead of you now,' said Isabel, joining them. 'It'll be great for you to live with your folks again. Here, write down your address for us, and make sure you keep in touch.'

Soon everyone was crowding round, asking for Hilary's address and Janet joked, 'You're going to have writer's cramp, with all the people you've promised to keep in touch with, Hilary. Oh, here are the coaches! Come on, girls! Time we made a move.'

Picking up their hand luggage, the girls made their way down to the big hall, where many of the younger girls and some of the mistresses were already gathered.

'Hilary!' called out Miss Harry. 'I'm glad to have this chance to say goodbye. It was nice to have you in my class, if only for one term.'

'And it was nice to be there, Miss Harry,' Hilary said.

'*Ma chère* Hilary!' cried Mam'zelle, tears gathering in her eyes as she enveloped the girl in a great hug. 'Be happy. We shall miss you.'

'And I'll miss you, Mam'zelle,' Hilary gulped, hoping that she wasn't going to cry.

Miss Theobald, coming out of her study at that moment, saw the girl's lips begin to tremble and went across. 'My dear,' she said warmly, taking her hand. 'Go forward into your new life with many happy memories of us . . . as we have of you. And remember, a little part of you will always remain here, in the spirit of St Clare's.'

'Thank you, Miss Theobald. I'm so proud to have been here, to have known you – Mam'zelle – everyone . . .' Suddenly Hilary couldn't speak any more for the lump in her throat.

'Hilary, come on! We'll miss the coach.' Pat came up then and took her arm. 'Oh, excuse me, Miss Theobald.'

'It's all right, Pat,' said the head. 'Goodbye, Hilary.'

'Goodbye, Miss Theobald.'

And goodbye, St Clare's, thought Hilary, as she walked outside – away from the school she loved so much – and into a new life.

Enid Blyton™

First Term at

Malory Towers

Darrell's off to her new school.
But what has she packed?
1. Tennis racket? ✓
2. Pocket-money? ✓
3. A lid for her temper? ✗
Oh dear! Malory Towers has a
trunkload of trouble to come!

There's Mischief at
Malory Towers

Enid Blyton™

Second Form at

Malory Towers

This year, Belinda has
a talent for drawing,
Alicia has a talent for tricks
and someone has a
talent for stealing purses . . .

There's Mischief at Malory Towers

Enid Blyton

Third Year at Malory Towers

And they're off!
Saddle up for a wild term
with Darrell and her friends.
There's so much going on!
Will they make it
past the finish line?

There's Mischief at Malory Towers

Enid Blyton™

Upper Fourth AT

Malory Towers

For starters, there's
twin trouble with Connie and Ruth.
The main pain is Gwen.
To finish, there's a picnic and a
midnight feast in a thunderstorm.

There's Mischief AT Malory Towers

Enid Blyton™

In the Fifth at Malory Towers

The Fifth Year presents:

Cinderella — written by Darrell

Alicia as the Demon King

Gwen (or will it be Maureen?)
as Cinderella.

There'll be drama before
the curtain even goes up!

There's Mischief at Malory Towers